The Case of the Haematophagous Equine

Rhiannon D. Elton

The Case of the Haematophagous Equine © Rhiannon D. Elton 2022
The Wolflock Cases: Book 8
Second edition

ISBN: 978-0-6487636-7-3 (paperback)

First Edition published July 2017
Second Edition published March 2022

info@rhiannoneltonauthor.com

Cover compiled by Rhiannon D. Elton

Cataloguing-in-Publication information for this title is listed with the National Library of Australia.

Published in Australia by Rhiannon D. Elton and Pelaia Adventures

This project is supported by the Regional Arts Development Fund (RADF). RADF is a partnership between the Queensland Government and Logan City Council to support arts and culture in regional Queensland.

*Dedicated to Helen & Nicholas Crowley,
Your support from the very beginning brought me to
here. Knowing I needed to get these written for you
was often the push I needed.*

Get More of the Magic & Mystery...

subscribe.rhiannoneltonauthor.com/more

If you want more clues, more magic and more mystery, let me know by going to the Wolflock Cases subscribe page.

You'll get clues, maps, sketches, behind the scenes stories, lore and much more! You'll also be the first to know when a new story is coming out so you can solve the mystery before your friends.

If you sign up with the magical link below, you'll also get a free downloadable map to follow Wolflock's journey to Mystentine University.

subscribe.rhiannoneltonauthor.com/more

Declaration of Intention

Merry meet,

The purpose of the books the author writes is to give representation to as many peoples, creatures and landscapes as they can. Although written from the perspective of a Caucasian teenage boy, the author hopes to offer a light into the harmony of different cultures and creeds of people. The author's aim is to promote harmony, understanding and compassion in all areas, while also inspiring readers to stand up against injustice and be critical thinkers in life.

While the author does their best to research, interview and highlight the best parts of people, they are only human and can make mistakes. The author asks you gently educate them by sending them an email in order to discuss anything that may have caused harm to a group of people unintentionally.

The author believes that the cure for ignorance is education, but please approach the topic cordially in order to avoid any knee-jerk cognitive dissonance.

Finally, the viewpoints displayed in the books comes from a particular character and is not necessarily that of the author's. The author seeks to display flaws, growth and human nature on many levels, and hopes that you will analyse the character of the protagonist without adopting any negative behaviours from them.

Merry part, and merry meet again.

CHAPTER 1

False Start

Wolflock had never seen Mothy's eyes change colour before. He'd only ever seen that they had changed. He looked with desperation into his best friend's face. At any moment, he expected the weight of their situation to hit him and for the terror he felt to be reflected.

Mothy's tired grey-blue eyes blinked up at him as he untwisted from the blanket. He still moved too slowly for Wolflock's liking. Perhaps he hadn't understood him.

"We've missed the carriage," he repeated, unable to keep a crackle from bubbling out of his throat.

Mothy's bottom lip protruded in thought and his eyes sank into a hazel apathy. He melted back into the blankets and covered his face from the midday sunlight.

"M-Mothy?"

"What?" he groaned.

"We've missed the-"

"We'll just get the next one. Why are you awake? I'm sore. Go back to sleep."

Dr Qwan snorted and pulled his shoes on. "Ah yes. The life of the young. Sleep all day, party all night. Rinse and repeat until age throws you a sign to stop."

"Age never stopped you." Charmainette tapped her foot at the door, glancing down the stairs to their sitting room doorway.

"Ah, my precious flame. I blame that entirely on the vitality of my good medicine and energetic wife." He pecked her cheek as he passed downstairs, loudly greeting his patient. "Merry meet to you, Mr Jorgen. You look how I should feel. Let's get you a nice thick remedy and get you back home before the children notice, eh?"

As they spoke, Wolflock tried to find his shoes, throwing pillows and blankets everywhere. Shoes and satchel. That was all he needed. Surely, they had to be here somewhere.

"Ahem," Charmainette coughed, jerking her

thumb at the hooks on the wall beside the door.

On it hung his shoes, laced over one hook, and his satchel bag.

"I picked them up as we came in. Your friend was using one as a sleep toy."

"Thanks. Mothy, for goodness sake! Mothy, get up!" Wolflock tugged his shoes on and tied them, throwing another pillow at the cocooned Mothy.

"We can't do anything until we get another carriage. Let me sleep," he groaned.

"You are so obstinate! What if it had to stop for maintenance? Or if they're waiting for us? Or if it's delayed? I'm leaving you here. If you don't make it to the carriage in time, I'm going to Mystentine without you."

Mothy stayed still and silent.

With a frustrated huff, Wolflock charged out of the room and out the front door.

The overcast sky did not dull the bright light, but seemed more cutting. Wolflock squinted around to gather his bearings before taking off North down the main road. Tourists and townsfolk milled about, drying fish on racks, and smoking them in outdoor ovens, while children played with the tangled decorations. No one seemed to be working, which irritated Wolflock even more as they chose to casually block the streets he needed to run down.

His heart tried to strangle him as he pushed through the sleepy crowds, tearing his way along the stony roads to the North Gatehouse Stables. Like yesterday, he flung open the doors and hurled himself towards the counter where the youth from yesterday snored, his mousy brown mop of hair on his hands.

Wolflock slammed his hands on the desk by his head, causing the boy to jump awake. "Our carriage! From yesterday! Is it still here?"

The boy blinked his red eyes at Wolflock as if he were some strange apparition. "Two-too?" he yawned. At least he had some skills of recollection. "Nah. Gone. Fella waited over two hours for you and your friend. Had to get going, though. Sorry. Next carriage is booked to come in next week though. It's a cargo one. Won't be comfy sorry."

His square jaw and constant apologising grate against Wolflock.

"There has got to be some other way. Is there a carriage in town we can buy? Or a smaller one used for local transport?"

"Nah, sir. Sorry. You've come at a terrible time for gettin' to the city. Most folks stay here 'til the end of the season and go to Mystentine just a'fore the Winter.

Traffic has a flow, ya know?"

"Please tell me there is something!" Wolflock scanned the boy's face, hoping for any sign or clue he could use to leverage the transport he needed.

The dullard shook his head, not even giving it a thought. "Sorry, sir. You're gonna just have to wait or organise private transport with someone in town."

Wolflock felt two sensations he was unfamiliar with, yet had experienced only a handful of times before. The first was a cold, sinking feeling of helplessness and disappointment, verging on devastation. The second was a sharp flash of pain through his skull.

Not wanting to let the attendant see him wince in pain, he turned and dragged his feet from the building. The light didn't help his headache, but he didn't know where else to go. Part of him wanted to curl up into a ball and disappear. Another part wanting to rage down the street screaming for someone to help him. He chose at least trying the former.

He sat on the stairs and wrapped his arms around his legs, pressing his face into his knees to block out the glaring sunlight. The carriage boy was right. Barely any foot traffic made its way this far to the edge of town and not a single person in sight looked ready to leave. He glared at them as they meandered back and forth, swapping food dishes and trinkets, fawning over children throwing tantrums from staying out too late.

Fools. Don't any of them see I'm upset? At this rate, we'll not even make it to Mystentine at all and we'll have to stay in this awful fishing town all Winter. Perhaps I can go back to the Silver Ice Hair... No. That would be worse. I'll never go back to Plugh if I can help it.

He felt someone flop next to him on the stairs and drape themselves over him.

"No luck, Lockie?"

"No."

"Maybe you can use your powers of princely status to charm someone over breakfast. Dr Qwan wants to take us to a place that sells the best late breakfast in Creast," Mothy sighed, leaning heavily on the sulking Wolflock.

"It's not like there is anything else to do. Do you know where this eatery is located?"

"Nope. I thought you could deduce that. I told Dr Qwan we'd meet him there."

Wolflock stayed silent for a moment, his face still pressed to his knees. If he could pinch the bridge of his nose in mild frustration, he would have, but Mothy's weight squashed him down.

"You know I'm not a homing pigeon, aye?"

"Oh, I know. I just like to set you up with little

challenges, so you feel clever. Using that noggin' of yours always puts you in a better mood."

Wolflock sighed again. He wasn't wrong.

"And who knows? Maybe we'll fall into the lap of the biggest puzzle to solve, and you'll have the best day ever."

"Highly unlikely. What information do you have about this restaurant?"

Mothy stretched off Wolflock and got to his feet like a marionette being inexpertly operated. "I know it's a small café that has the only steamed buns in Creast. Possibly even all of Shiriling."

"All this information from Dr Qwan himself?"

"His wife said it's a pokey little café that serves more land meats than fish."

Wolflock slumped and then forced himself to his feet, letting Mothy drag him back to where he thought Dr Qwan's house was. It wasn't easy to find again, but the smell of the medicinal herbs they burned and boiled was pungent enough to stand out from the cooking fish throughout town. When they arrived, Wolflock gazed around at the streets. One led downhill to the bay, one uphill to the Eastern border of town, and one to the North.

"Dr Qwan has shown himself to have enough

foresight to not want to climb a hill before he has eaten." He pointed up the hill. "Nor after he is full." He pointed to the bay. "His café is likely to be in this direction. Keep your nose alert for anything that doesn't smell like fish."

The boys walked along the cobblestone street, crossing three lanes and following their noses down an alley. Mothy pointed out an A-frame sign, pointing them toward a café. Wolflock also pointed out the decorative edges of the sign engraved with Xiayahn letters.

"Ah yes. Not a language I'm familiar with, but never-the-less, they do a mean breakfast bun. C'mon boys." Dr Qwan tapped both their shoulders, having listened to their deductions. "No luck with the cart, Mr Wolflock Felen?"

Wolflock sighed through his nose. "No. You wouldn't know anyone who would have a spare carriage, would you? I'll pay handsomely for it."

"Have some food first. I'll think when this hangover ebbs."

The boys sat in sturdy, hand carved wooden chairs with fur lined cushions. A young boy with Xiayahn almond eyes and brown curly hair served them hot lemon water and honey while they waited for Dr Qwan to order for them at the counter. The café was a hole in a wall, but it had a cozy charm that brought indoor items to the outdoors, making the space feel larger.

Dr Qwan and an older gentleman conversed thick and fast in two different Xiayahn dialects. Wolflock listened and heard distinct notes in their cadences as well as favoured words. Dr Qwan made sharper ends to his words, whereas the cafe owner drew theirs out in a longer drawl. He also heard the universal tones of someone saying, "I don't know that word. Is this closer?"

Mothy ran his fingers over his edge of the table and found a board game in a compartment on their table and drew it out, making up his own game for how the pieces moved and beating himself in a spectacular fashion.

"Well, that's it. I've lost the farm. Better move onto ship work," he sighed, shaking his head in defeat.

"Farm work didn't suit you, anyway. Why not run away and join the circus?" Wolflock offered, sipping his tea.

Mothy leaned back in his chair and pondered the idea. "Well... there is that. I could always join a temple. The Temples of Love or the Arts always caught my eye."

"Mmm... It may be quite different here in Shiriling. Arts here seem a bit more... rustic. To put it politely."

"I wouldn't call it polite," Mothy snickered.

"We may have to spend a few months in a temple

if we don't make it to the mountain in time."

"What one would you pick?"

"Do they have a temple for knowledge and wisdom?"

"Pfft. You have neither until you've had your education. But then again... maybe they'd make an exception for you. I'd probably want to go into a Life temple so I can learn their medicine and midwifery techniques."

"Still on track to become a doctor?"

Mothy grinned and glanced at Dr Qwan as he brought over a tray of pastries, buns and dried meat strips. "Being able to see Dr Qwan's pharmacy last night inspired me even more than helping Nu cure the ship. The functions of the body and how it responds to medicine is just so fascinating! And it's not just chemicals either. Different points can create different responses and things that are within people's control can make a big difference. Like this!"

Mothy leaned over the table, knocking a few pieces from his imaginary board game that clattered to the floor. He gripped Wolflock's hand and jammed his knuckle into the thick webbing between his thumb and index finger.

"Ouch! Why does that hurt? Gah! Mothy!"

Wolflock tried to struggle free, but Mothy focused his bright green eyes on the spot and drove his knuckle into it with tiny circles.

"Ah. Good lad. Gi Chuan. Big Mound. Frees the Qi of the channels throughout the body and rules the head and face." Dr Qwan placed the tray down and served up three plates of the unique foods. A perfect blend of the harsh, tundra bound foods of Shiriling, and the colourful fullness of Xiayah.

"How is your headache?" Mothy grinned.

Wolflock returned his attention to his aching temples and blinked. "It's gone."

"It's like magic! Aye?"

Wolflock thought hard, searching for the headache, but he couldn't find a trace of pain left. "That's a nifty trick. You're a natural healer, Mothy. Now only my hand hurts."

"Not as bad as having a headache, though. Especially for someone whose head is as full as yours."

"There is definitely no room for pain. Are we to guess what this food is or are you going to inform us of the menu you've prescribed for today, Dr Qwan?"

"You spoil my fun, Mr Wolflock Felen. I have one over you, though. These buns are all filled with different fillings, yet the outside is identical. We have pork curry buns, egg buns, hare buns, and ginger vegetable medley buns. We also have a mild side serving of sweet fried chicken and egg noodles."

"It would be better to have venison, but this man keeps insulting the butcher and pretending to be me!" The café owner waved a spatula towards them, overhearing their conversation from the counter.

"But you two look nothing alike," said Mothy.

Wolflock agreed to himself as he looked over at them. The café owner's eyes drooped at the edges and his hairline receded high on his head, making his round face more moon-like. Besides their smooth upper eyelids and black hair, the two men looked vastly different.

"He wears an apron he stole from me last year."

"Stole is such a strong word. I just keep forgetting to return it." Dr Qwan stuffed a bun into his mouth. "Besides, the butcher keeps saying I'm unqualified because you keep telling him raw eggs is medicine."

"Again... why would he believe that?" Wolflock drawled.

"He says it while he's wearing my old lab coat. He borrowed for a fancy dress party."

The boys looked at each other and chuckled. The older men bantered for longer until Dr Qwan delivered a back-handed compliment about how they needed to enjoy the beautiful food, not the terrible company.

Wolflock watched the street out of the alley, hoping more patrons would find their way to the café and he could interrogate them about transport. No one appeared, though. No one even ventured down the street. Each moment gnawed away his hope.

"Lockie," Mothy broke into his spiral, "eat some food. It's fantastic."

"I'm not feeling hungry."

"Yes, you are. You've got that anxious, hungry look on your face. Take a bite and tell me I'm wrong."

Wolflock turned back to the table and picked up a bun. He gave it a squeeze and felt a soft centre. Rolling his eyes, he took a large bite and swallowed. The soft bun bounced in his mouth and the surge of flavours rushed through his face. The delicious ginger and chicken mince surprised him, and his stomach unknotted enough to grumble that it was hungry. As he continued eating the warm cuisine, he felt grateful Mothy didn't point out that he had been right.

His gut settled, and Wolflock felt his mind clear. Dr Qwan showed them how to play the board game Mothy had found while they ate, but the boys decided they liked Mothy's version better. It had far more interesting rules, such as, every third turn you get to move one of the opponent's pieces, and if you stacked pieces you could end up with a super tower, but if shaking the table toppled them, they were lost forever.

Midway through their fourth game, a gang of urchin children ran down the alley. The eldest, whom Wolflock recognised from the geode cracking stall yesterday, heaved a bag of coins onto the café counter.

"Round of mystery buns, thanks, Hwa."

The café owner checked the coins. As he removed them, Wolflock saw they were all sentus coins.

"You keep paying me in small change. I'm going to build a house out of these." He waved the wooden circle as if it were a threat.

"And we will gladly fund it as long as we get those buns. The tide's goin' out soon, so we need more energy."

"Wasabi crab buns coming." Hwa turned back and loaded up a wooden steamer tower with dozens of fluffy buns.

The other children pushed and shoved one another for cushions on a large piece of carpet in the alleyway, establishing the pecking order between them for the meal. The ringleader walked away from the counter but caught Wolflock's eye before they made it to their cushion.

"Oh? What's this then? Merry meet, Mister. You look bloody awful."

Wolflock had sunk into his chair so deeply his chin rested on his chest. His unbrushed hair hung bedraggled around his face, and the dark bags under his eyes hadn't lifted with food. He also hadn't changed clothes overnight and so his normally pristine white shirt and sleek jacket were stained with food, salt and still smelled of fish.

"I'm sure the doctor said something about youth letting you have an advantage over us oldies," he groaned as he straightened up.

"You ain't that old, are ya? I s'pose ya must be to know about rocks and stuff like ya do."

"You know about them and you're not old," he retorted.

"Mmm... that's fair." They hummed, tucking a thick golden lock of hair under their grey hood. "How long are ya in town for?"

"Seeing how long you have to worry about me giving your secrets away?"

The child's face scrunched, and they avoided eye contact.

"Well, our carriage left before we could get to it, so, if you know a way to get to Mystentine today, your secret will leave with us."

They pouted as they thought, turning their head this way and that. Wolflock ate through a pork bun as he observed them. Tall and gangly, with a youthful face, he guessed they were around eleven. A practical person with access to very sturdy materials made the weathered grey coat and hood. A little copper bracelet around their wrist had a heart and an anchor and, although it had tinged their skin with green, they still wore it. The pocket of their thick cotton trousers had a damp patch and a cloth poking out of it, which explained why all the children's faces were clean. They also showed no cuts, bruises, limping, or torn clothes. They didn't get into any scuffs.

This child was the parental figure for the other urchin children in town and they had to grow up quickly as their own parent was likely out at sea on a hunting vessel or a long-distance trade ship.

"Nup. Got nothing. If the stables don't have a ride for you, then I guess you're out of luck."

Wolflock smiled. He knew how to get them thinking.

"That's a shame. I really thought you could help."

"Why'd you think that?" the child looked at him sideways with an air of suspicion.

"Well, you were very enterprising with the geode stall. It's a good little gig. I bet you've saved up lots of money and that makes your dad proud. I'd wager he comes back from his work on boats and brings you the best presents for doing such a good job."

He ran a risk saying "father" and not mother, but a twitch in the corner of their mouth confirmed he'd guessed right.

"You look after all the other kids every day and I'm sure they feel like family. You'd do anything for them, right?"

"We're all we have most days. So yeah. Dunno how this means I could have helped, though."

"If any of them needed help from Mystentine, I thought you'd have a backup plan to make sure they got there faster than anyone else in town. Do you have something like that?"

The child thought to themselves, looking at Dr Qwan's chair leg, then they paled.

"I mean..."

"Hah! You do! Excellent! Tell me. Tell me how to get to where we need to go!"

The child shook their head. "Nah. Mister. You don't want that. Like... it's good if you're so sick ya can't 'member nothin'. It ain't good for normal travel."

Wolflock laid his hand on the table flat. "Listen. I will go through any torment to get to Mystentine before the cold seals off the mountain. I will travel amongst potato sacks or smelly goats. I'll sit squished between sweaty, foul-mouthed mercenaries. As long as I don't have to go back to Plugh."

The child picked at their ear as they waited for him to finish. "If ya go with Khra, you'll wish ya were travelling with all of those times ten."

Wolflock didn't break eye contact, waiting.

"Well... if ya say so, Mister. Khra lives outside the North side of the city. You go out the gates, turn to the water and keep walking around the edge of the woods until you find a cave. If they ain't on a job, they'll be there. Make sure ya don't have no open wounds when you go, though."

Mothy and Wolflock both frowned at the last remark.

"Why that specifically?"

"Because Khra ain't no normal driver. He'll suck your soul out through any cut in ya skin. He's a demon."

CHAPTER 2

Dark Deals

ilence hit the cafe. The children all stopped babbling at once. Even Dr Qwan stopped mid-bite into a mystery steam bun.

Wolflock held his features in place as he saw the child was looking at him for a reaction.

Was this a prank? What were they playing at? Mentioning demons was serious business. It wasn't something a young child should have been aware of, let alone be throwing around like the name of a local bully.

"What do you mean, demon?" he asked.

"I said what I said, didn't I? Don't make me say it

again. That's what summons it. All you've gots to do is to say its name, right? Then it comes out of the darkness to steal little kids."

The children on the carpet all gasped in fright, shirking away from their leader. Wolflock thought it was ironic that this child didn't think they were part of the "little" children.

"But they are a functioning form of transportation, are they not?" he asked, wondering if this was just local folklore or a misunderstood hermit. The likelihood of a true demon living this close to town was inconceivable.

"I've given you directions. Don't ask me nothing more about it!"

Wolflock couldn't quite tell if him not showing any concern about the possibility of the driver being a demon had upset the child more, but they huffed and moved towards the carpet to be with their friends. As they turned, he asked one final question.

"How do you know about this?"

The child looked back over their shoulder. Their face was still pale from having to divulge the information in the first place. "I hear things, don't I? All of them people who don't want the guard seeing their business. It all starts at the docks and strings through town like dog slobber. All the ones who have mean business to do, they all ask for...

Khra."

As they spoke, Wolflock got to his feet, collecting his things.

"Mothy, it looks like we may have our driver. Let's go."

Mothy had already started collecting steam buns in a large cloth and tucked them safely in the top of his bag. Dr Qwan also got to his feet.

"I best show you boys the way to the gate. This food always leaves me in a mental food coma if I eat too much, and this is a good time to stop."

The café owner yelled across the counter in his Xiayahn dialect as they departed.

"When do I not pay my bill?" Dr Qwan answered in common Puinteylien.

The three of them continued leaving as the café owner began clearly listing things in their native language. Wolflock had left a few deimas on the table to stop Mothy from trying to pay.

As they headed along the Northern roads to the gate, Wolflock asked Dr Qwan, "Do you know anything about this mysterious Khra? Are the rumours the children presented to us true?"

Dr Qwan pursed his lips in thought. "There might be. I've never needed their services. Charmainette and I prefer to go on foot. Or I borrow my brother's transport. I save up all my long-distance doings until he comes to visit."

The only folk they saw at the fifteen feet high walls were the two guards playing cards under the walkway above the open portcullis. The guards paid them very little heed, only nodding as they passed.

Before they passed through, all of them jumped at the sound of a bear roaring behind them in the town. They turned to see not a bear, but Charmainette, charging at them, her wild red hair tied in a tight bun.

"WHERE DO YOU THINK YOU'RE GOING?" She wielded her doctor's bag with a fury that would knock over forests. "YOU SAID YOU WOULD WORK TODAY! WHERE HAVE YOU BEEN?"

"Oh, I'm sorry, my love," Dr Qwan beamed, trying to embrace his wife. "Our guests missed their carriage and I've been helping them find a new way to get to Mystentine. Far be it from me to stop such promising students from pursuing their studies."

"Far be it from you to cancel all your patients at the last minute to go eat alley food!"

"It was just a little snack, my dove. These boys are skin and bone. I was just going to send them on their way and be right back."

"Oh, no you won't! Get back to the clinic now!"

"I need to show them how to get to-"

"Have you been given directions to where you need to go?" Charmainette cut across her husband, addressing the boys directly.

Wolflock nodded. "Yes. We can find the way."

"Good! Thank you for all you have done in Creast, but my husband is needed and, if he's given a minute, he'll take a day. I haven't had a day off in a month and you are taking all my patients for the next week." She linked arms with Dr Qwan and began dragging him away.

"Ah! Torch to my soul. I am enchanted by your passion. I love the way you fill my day with fireworks. Good luck, boys. I must soothe the blaze of an overworked woman. Merry part."

Mothy elbowed Wolflock in the arm as he protested.

"We'll be fine. Merry part and merry meet again!" He then turned to Wolflock. "I'm sure a bright appraising investigator such as yourself doesn't need any help finding a shady carriage driver with the instructions that kid gave us."

The doctor gave a cheerful wave back at them and left them in silence with the two guards. The four of them made eye contact, shrugged, and went back to their business.

Outside the gate, the boys turned so the outer wall stayed on their right and the woodlands to their left. The wide field of brown grass and scattered mounds of snow marked their path. It remained clear of any trees and bushes, making their walk an easy one. Mothy waved to the occasional guard walking along the Creast town wall and kicked mounds of snow to see them scatter. He stopped kicking the mounds,though, when he saw a rabbit run under one, realising they might be dens for the wild creatures. But Wolflock's focus couldn't be broken from the task at hand, even for the allure of laughing with Mothy.

As they drew closer to the bay, they approached a large hill dividing them from the water.

"This must be part of the back of Jaxarna's mine. It may run for a good mile or so along the bay," Wolflock said, more to himself than to Mothy.

"I hope it does, and I hope it's filled with all the treasures her and Girid need," Mothy responded with a grin.

Wolflock saw his smile didn't reach his eyes as he looked up the hill. It was a long hike. "Don't worry. We're not going that way. See over there, by the treeline? There're mounds of snow that are kicked over like yours. Someone has been walking through there. Our path goes down that forest path, not up the hill."

"Oh, thank goodness!"

They trekked along the wide dirt road into the trees.

Wolflock's ear pricked as the noise of bugs and birds soon fell silent. The trees and hill protected the rich forest from the icy winds blowing off the bay, and, yet, there seemed to be no life. No rabbit or fox. Nothing.

It sent a chill through Wolflock's spine. Not even an insect. The branches of the tall pines loomed over them with their snow ladened branches diminishing the sunlight. The woods grew dark around them and, although he hummed a cheerful tune, Mothy walked close enough to bump into Wolflock's arm.

"I don't think I like this, Lockie."

Wolflock pressed on.

"Can't we just wait til next week? I'm sure we'll get a lovely carriage. I can learn at Dr Qwan's clinic, and you can watch the people on the dock and learn about them. You like that, right?"

His steps slowed. They'd been walking for a long time. Had they missed a fork in the road? The child had told him to turn to the bay, right?

"Do you want to work in a temple for the next four months or more?" he shot a cold look at his friend.

"I really don't care either way. I would just like to be able to keep working at all. No point getting to Mystentine if it's in a coffin."

Wolflock huffed, but his footsteps slowed.

"Just a bit further. I think I can make out fresh carriage tracks. Let's make it to that big birch tree, and then we'll see if we can find anything."

They walked in a palpable silence. Every step made the hair on the back of their necks prickle and, even without saying it, they felt as if something was watching them. The moment they reached the birch tree, Mothy sprang around to walk back.

"We made it. No one's here. Let's go."

As Mothy spoke Wolflock could have sworn he heard something. He gripped Mothy's arm and froze. Then he heard it again. A thick crunching, grinding noise. His eyes slid to his right and saw it; a clearing against the hill that was only sixty feet away and a large black carriage. Without a word, he stepped down the path to the clearing.

Throughout the clearing lay disorganised broken pieces of debris, as well as old bric-à-brac and disused carriage repair tools. Amongst them, he couldn't see any footprints or shoe prints, but he could see the deep intents of hooves that came to a point. He turned to Mothy to show him, but that sense of someone watching caught the words in his throat. Wolflock knelt to run his hand over old hammers, lathes, and a sanding block. The tools had strange patterns of damage to the wooden handles; a deep indent that had caused splintering in the wood where a large hand would have gripped at the pinkie and index fingers. The tins of polish were spilled over the ground, staining the leaves black. The old, empty tins were dented, and one looked as if a bear had torn it open. But, that wasn't the only odd thing about the rubbish left in the clearing.

The water and food troughs for the horses were bone dry. Wolflock touched the old pine wood, greyed and splitting from age, and found holes in the bottom from where the troughs were in much need of repair.

The carriage itself had an odd hitching system. Normally, belts would go around the horse and fasten to the carriage shaft. The only pieces present were the collar and a rigid half saddle strap. This contraption seemed to allow the horse to have full autonomy to decide if it wanted the harness on or not, which was dangerous, because, if it became spooked, it would free itself and leave the carriage in danger. Besides all that, a carriage this size should have had space for at least four horses to move it. Wolflock could only see it was equipped with one place for a horse. The collar suggested it was a very large horse, but still not enough to pull the full weight of such a large vehicle.

Besides the odd mechanics of the carriage, it was in terrible condition. The black paint was peeled all over it and he couldn't see through the windows because of the frosting of grime over them. The only things that seemed to be in fair condition were the wheels. Old, and made from expert artisans, they had recently been oiled and checked for defects, as he could tell by their shine.

The crunching noise grew louder, startling him from his thoughts.

"Ahem. Merry meet?" he called out.

Mothy attacked him with a flurry of slaps along his arm, shushing him. "Can't you smell that?" he breathed, turning pale.

Wolflock sniffed the air and took a step closer to the cave backed into the hillside, curtained with the roots and dangling branches of a snow willow above it. An acrid smell of iron and salt emanated from the cave.

"It's blood," Mothy mouthed.

"I beg your pardon, Driver Khra. We were hoping to employ your services." The anxiety of not getting to Mystentine in time to reach the university overpowered the instinct to run as he called out again. The crunching stopped and an enormous creature shuffled around in the darkness. "You came highly recommended, and we need to get to Mystentine city with all due urgency."

Laboured breathing was the only response.

"I don't mind being a few hours late to Mystentine, but, if we have to wait any longer, we're going to be too late to get to the university. I have plenty of deimas for when the job is done. What say you?" Wolflock tapped his foot irritably. Being so spooked made him mad. Even more so since the stranger wouldn't reveal themselves.

"Payment... up front..." wheezed a voice that sounded both shrill and throaty at the same time. Wolflock jerked back. It sounded so familiar, yet like fresh snapping icicles.

"Uh... What is your price for a one-way trip to Mystentine?"

The creature came closer to the roots, its rapid pants breathing a putrid meat smell through the veil. "The lion... the butcher's... daughter... hunted this morning." An unearthly voice grunted in low tones, snorting and panting.

"That's it? And you can get us to Mystentine before the end of the month? We'll need at least two or three days to climb the mountain."

"What day is it?" the voice rumbled low.

"There was a full moon last night, so it must be the sixteenth of Nibit'ling Ickst. We need to get to Mystentine by the morning of the twenty-sixth. That's ten days." Wolflock waved his fingers as the math shot like lightning through his mind.

"Five... days..."

"You can get us there in seven days?" He blinked. No horse could move that fast, let alone while pulling a carriage of that size alone.

"Five... days..." the voice repeated with another shrill note at the end of its words.

Wolflock had never heard a voice quite like it. Not that he could remember, at least. Curiosity itched at him, and he stepped closer to the roots, looking up into the darkness. He heard the creature suck in and hold its breath as if it were savouring the smell of him. Wolflock felt his body quiver uncontrollably as the urge to run as fast as he could filled his body. A thick breath filled with rot and iron washed over him. The angle it came from pushed his hair down. Whatever the creature was, it stood at least seven feet tall and two blood-red eyes stared unblinkingly down at him, obscured by clumps of greasy, tangled hair.

"Are you Khra?"

The red eyed being above him drew another long breath and held it.

"Yes," they hissed a slow answer.

Wolflock heard that odd shrill note in their deep throaty voice and again he thought he'd heard it somewhere else. He stepped a little closer. He could tell Khra wasn't human. That much was obvious. But morbid fascination mixed with fear pushed him to solve the mystery of what this thing was.

"If that's all," Mothy squeaked as he grabbed

Wolflock's arm and pulled him back, "we'll be heading off to get your payment. If we aren't back, well... It just wasn't meant to be then, aye? Merry part!"

Wolflock's piercing blue eyes watched the red ones disappear behind the veil as Mothy jogged them away. He didn't let go of his friend's arm or let up their speed until they were back in the clearing with the walls of Creast in view.

Neither of them realised how tightly they had been gripping one another's arm until they let go and a rush of pins and needles flooded them. Wolflock stared with wide eyes, feeling the pieces around the cave coming together in a new mental web, but the fear coursing through him refused to let them stick.

Mothy bent forward, panting with his hands on his thighs. "Shall we... try another demon carriage service... or is this one to your liking?"

"Have you ever seen a demon before?" Wolflock asked, catching his breath against a large boulder embedded in the field.

His friend shook his head, wiping his sweaty blonde hair from his forehead. "No. I saw someone nearly become one once, I think. Hazzim and I frequented the temple of fortune for business blessings and advice. Someone came in really sick once. I mean... It looked like their family had brought them in. Apparently, it's common for people suffering from greed to need the temple to help them. They seemed out of their mind. Screaming and shouting and snatching at anything shiny."

"That doesn't sound like what we just saw."

"You felt it though, right? It was sniffing you the same way I sniff for pie."

Wolflock pinched his chin between his thumb and index finger as they walked back into Creast. "I did. It seemed... hungry. And it was tall."

"I saw you look up. How tall?"

"Maybe seven feet? Maybe more."

"Seven feet? Seven feet! Lockie, we can't. Please tell me you have another plan. Can't we speak to Vanmoinen about using his elk? Or, what if we just wait? I'm sure working at the temples can't be that boring. It has to be better than being done away with by a monster... and you have that look in your eyes again."

Mothy's arms dropped, already defeated.

"Can you blame me? Solving a common folklore mystery with the promise of getting to Mystentine three days in advance with a carriage overflowing with dark and mysterious clues! Doesn't that sound like a much better trip than playing a hundred rounds of cards or toc-tic-tac all day?" Wolflock rubbed his hands together before taking off at a run. "Come now, Mothy, my friend. We haven't got all day."

As they drew closer to the gate, Mothy eyed him sourly. "You really are a magnet for trouble."

Rhiannon D. Elton

CHAPTER 3

Hunting the Huntress

As the boys came up to the gate, Wolflock ran up to the guards as one lost a game of cards, throwing down his hands and folding his arms.

"My good sirs, where can I find the butcher, whose daughter is a huntress?"

The guard who won scratched his head. "You mean the Slatra's?"

"Do you know any other butchers in town that have a huntress in their house?" the other guard snapped.

"What are you looking for Dorbi for, anyway?"

"Is that the huntress's name?" Mothy asked, eyeing

off their hands played on the table and the others scattered about.

"Yeah, s'right. Dorbi's our best huntress. Real gift for the forest she 'as. Never seen it thrive s'much as when she's been this edge's steward."

Wolflock didn't know how a huntress could make a forest thrive, but he didn't have time to ask. "Where is her shop? I must speak with her on a matter of great urgency."

"Well, you wanna go down the lane proper like," the winning guard pointed a stubby finger down the South Lane. "Then turn widdershins up the way, go past the park with the stage in it. If you hit the windmill, you've gone too far."

"If they get to the windmill, they're out of the wall, so of course they've gone too far." The losing guard rolled her eyes.

"It's just inside the gate to the Northwest, but you'll have to go South to get there. Can't miss it, really. Big space around it because of the smell, right?"

"Big space. Can't miss it. If you do, I don't think any directions would help."

Wolflock jogged on the spot before taking off again. "Northwest Gate. Got it."

As he ran, he heard Mothy call back, "Merry

thanks again!"

Wolflock kept to the main roads as he ran. He didn't know Creast well enough to not get stuck in dead end side lanes and blocked off short cuts. Without any problem, he found the butcher's shop in a large, paved area, at least one and a half houses from any other buildings. Fish drying on racks lined two thirds of it. Some apprentices in leather aprons stoked smokers on one side of the old building, while others scraped animal brains down racked deer skins on the other side.

All of them wore an oiled balaclava over their faces and Wolflock didn't have to wonder why for long. The breeze from the bay slowed for a moment and the full stench of the area hit him. Animal waste, blood, and decay washed over him like a putrid cloud, and he retched. Mothy laughed and pretended to savour the air as if it were a bed of flowers.

"That'll wake you up in the morning. Hazzim had a friend who would always say smelling that would put hair on your chest. I didn't know you could turn green, Lockie. What other talents have you been hiding from me?"

He continued to laugh as Wolflock ran into the butcher's shop. The shingle sign, shaped like a steak, swung above the entrance with Shirth words on it in ivory white that said "Slatrari Sounem".

The inside of the shop smelled completely different from the outside. Cool air blocked out the smoke and decay, replacing it with fresh rosemary, chipped ice and the smell of good quality, raw meat. A tall, barrel-built man with a chestnut beard stood on the other side of the counter, arguing in low tones with another man of similar stature.

Mothy politely began perusing the selection, but Wolflock paid no heed to the typical civilities. He marched up to the counter and slammed down twelve deimas.

"You. Away. He'll settle his gambling debts with you after he's given me what I need" he snapped at the bookie. "You. I need the mountain lion your daughter caught this morning. Now."

Both men stood flabbergasted and flushed red. Before they could speak, Wolflock rolled his eyes. "I know you're a bookie because of your jacket. You have three small paperback booklets on your person. I'd say you were effectively running an underground gambling ring. Dog shows, by the short hairs on your trousers. Small dogs, since they barely come up to your knee. The only dogs that are naturally this far north are the ones with long hair to deal with the cold. Although not illegal, the amount of people that you've permitted to gamble on dog shows would be, which is why you've got a second book tucked into the first. You also have an illegal drinking alcohol trade, which is why this man is keeping his shaking hands behind the counter. You knew you'd lose him as a customer and risk your entire ring by sending muscle in to claim back the debts, but, you knew by waving a bottle of your best under his nose he'd cave and at least give you something."

Wolflock could see Mothy grinning to himself as he checked over a string of sausages hanging from the rafters. The butcher blinked at him with an odd shade of violet in his eyes.

"You're doing it hard, though. It might be because Captain Jaimeron has cracked down on minor misdemeanours because of the stress the mayor has put him under, or it's because your best customer just lost all their mines and contacts and can no longer supply you with a strain of minor criminals."

"What's going on out here?"

The leather strip curtain behind the butcher flapped open as a knobbly old hand with nails like claws cut through. An old lady hobbled out, bent over her walking stick that was as knobbly as her. She looked up at Wolflock with shocking violet eyes. The wrinkles on her face looked like her tight bun was pulling them smoother over her bird-like face.

"Atral, who are these?"

"Customers, mor," The butcher withered away from the old woman, who didn't even look at him.

"And what are they buying?"

The butcher made a motion to the bookie to get him to play along. The other man stammered before picking up a hunk of venison.

"F-for dinner tonight," he said, plonking it down on the counter with a squishy slap sound.

"Excellent choice. Weigh and wrap the piece, Atral." Her voice had an elderly croak to it, but she commanded the room with a level of terror Wolflock had only seen from his father. The butcher took the meat and fumbled as he wrapped it, having to tie a large, messy knot as his hands wouldn't stop trembling. Wolflock also noticed he was sweating, even though it was cool in the shop.

"And how may we help you boys?" she asked Wolflock.

"We were here for the lion carcass your granddaughter hunted this morning. I'm sure the payment will help your son's gambling debts and drinking problem. I'm not sure how it goes in Creast, but in Plugh bookies only come to claim a debt when it's about fifty deimas-"

"Four pounds!" The butcher slapped the poorly wrapped meat in front of the bookie, cutting off Wolflock. "That'll be-"

The old woman held up her finger and her son fell silent. "How much will it be, Vloki?"

The bookie glanced back and forth from the old lady to her son, desperate for a hint at what he should say. Wolflock frowned, wondering why this old crone was so frightening to them.

"S-sixty deimas, ma'am."

She took his hand over the counter and patted it fondly. "You take this piece of meat worth all that, then. You take it and you enjoy it. Make sure you eat all of it."

"Y-yes ma'am." Wolflock and Mothy felt the tingle of cold prickle through the room as they watched the interaction.

"If you see my Atral in any place his mor would be disappointed to see him, you send him right home for me, won't you, Vloki?"

"Of course, ma'am." The bookie shivered, and his breath became fog.

"And that bottle in your pocket, you're going to give it to the doctor. You're going to give him the whole operation. That type of drink belongs to the professionals, like doctors and proper distillers, doesn't it?"

"O-of course, ma'am. It will be my gift to the town."

"Good man. Good man. You best be seeing that doctor soon then, eh?" Her face softened and the old crone looked grandmotherly.

"...Of course."

That little bit of hesitation from the bookie was all Wolflock needed to know he was lying. He might forgive the monetary debts, but he wasn't about to give away a lucrative operation, even if it was hurting people. The old woman seemed to think the same way.

"Just to make sure, then."

The man's teeth chattered, and ice crept up his hand clasped in the old woman's hands. He cried out and tried to pull it free, but the old woman held it like a vice until ice encapsulated half of his right arm. The bluish translucent ice quickly made his arm turn dark red, and he shouted in pain, tearing it away from her and rushing out the door.

"Go take Vloki his meat, Atral. All debts must be paid." The crone's creaky voice levelled out as she stared with no emotion at the door. Her son nodded nervously, scooped up the meat and ran, making the girl coming in jump to the side. "Now. How is it that you boys came to know about my Dorbi's lion before anyone else in town?"

"Our driver said that was all they'd take as payment for driving us to Mystentine on such short notice." Wolflock lifted his nose and brushed his nails against his shirt, trying to look nonchalant under the old woman's gaze.

They both held a long silence, Wolflock glancing around but keeping the old woman in his peripheries, and the old woman staring at him with bored, half-lidded eyes. Mothy bounced on the balls of his feet, looking ready to run.

"Farmor? What is this?" asked the granddaughter. She could have only been only a year older than Wolflock and Mothy, given the approximate age of her father, but she stood half a foot taller than both of them and had a thick set, sturdy build.

"These boys want your lion."

"It's for Khra," Mothy blurted out. "They have the only carriage left in Creast that can get us to Mystentine before the Winter blocks the pass up the mountain!"

Wolflock turned slowly to Mothy with wide eyes and an expression that demanded to know why he played their hand.

"Sorry! The demon left me frightened."

"Old Khra, huh?" The old lady scratched her bony chin. After a moment, she waved her hand, and the room chilled, filling with glittering shards of ice and snow. "Watch the shop, Dorbi. I'll discuss business with these boys."

"Farmor, I was hoping to have this one for-"

The old lady just looked at the tall girl with that piercing stare.

"I'll watch the shop."

"Follow me." The old crone waved at the boys, beckoning them through the leather strip curtain.

As they passed through, Wolflock felt the clean sheen of polish over the leather and smelt the pine oil used to sterilise it. The three of them moved through a clean, cold stone room with hanging meats and a workbench, and into a hallway that led them to the back room and kitchen. Wolflock could tell the house was what he would consider "old" money. Out of style, but with high-quality carpet, rugs and wallpaper that faded around them. Old paintings of hunters conquering beasts and hand carved wooden furniture filled the house, and, yet, the paint and wood cracked from both age and lack of knowledge on how to preserve it.

On the hallway tables glittered dusty crystals and

books about advanced magic, and a besom stood in the corner, decorated with black ribbons, shells and black beads.

"Sit." The old woman took her place, sitting at the head of the table in their stoneware kitchen.

The boys followed the instruction, Mothy sitting closest to the back door. His face showed a polite smile, but his knee bounced as if he were ready to run. The old woman remained silent, watching them with her bored stare. Wolflock drummed his fingers on the daintily laid out table. The Slatra family had also hit difficult times; he could see by the way the tablecloth and runner draped into folds on the floor, and the way the doily placemats butted up against each other, some overlapping. All here had been suited to a much larger table. The size of the external house suggested there was space for a proper dining room, but the cost of heating the area must have been too great, or they had to sell the original table and move everything into the kitchen where the staff would eat.

Glittering on every inch of the exposed walls were dozens of necklaces and large gemstones tied in leather strings, all in different shapes and sizes. Was the old woman a collector? There didn't seem to be much of a pattern between them.

"I will give you the lion for the twelve deimas," Wolflock's shoulders relaxed, but the old woman continued, "but, knowing you are to give it to the one known as Khra comes at an extra cost."

"Which is?"

The old woman smacked her lips around her gums. "My sister vanished, along with my husband. I want you to find what happened to them. The last place I saw her was at a little hamlet on the road to Mystentine called Restöfundsjúkum."

"Does that have a translation?" Mothy swallowed.

"Resting Bones."

Something about the nasty smirk the old woman had across her crinkled face made Wolflock uneasy. "And when were they last seen at Restöfundsjúkum?"

A menacing grin split across her cruel face. "Forty years ago."

CHAPTER 4
Bangle & Blutro

olflock's eyes narrowed at the old woman. "I will require some clarification. You want me to find out what happened to your sister and husband over forty years ago in a poky little hamlet? In the same region that was ravaged by war for five years over a decade ago?"

"That's what the lion is worth. My Dorbi risked her life for it, and I'll not cheapen it. Twelve deimas to lay claim to it and the information about my sister and husband in order to give it to the dark one."

"Dark one?" Mothy asked as he fiddled with the

hem of a doily.

"Oh yes. The one who never walks in the light, with eyes that burn like hot coals. A creature that only accepts the darkest of passengers. The same driver who drives my husband's carriage."

"Wait. That tattered old black carriage is yours?"

"No. It was my husband's. He worked for the old Hunter's Guild; I don't know if they're still operating. If they are, they don't have many members left. I don't know how the dark one got hold of it. I had to leave Shiriling when the war came. When I came back, the carriage had resurfaced and was in use. I tried approaching the man who drove it to ask about it, but that horse is the fastest I've ever known. It was obvious he wouldn't talk to me. I wrote letters to him with no response. I wrote letters asking after my sister and my husband, and still, nothing."

"Did they ever write to you?" Wolflock asked, pinching his chin.

The old woman rose to her feet and drew out an old tin box from the back of their pantry. "These were all I had. They stopped the night my husband left on a mission."

"Do you know why he left that night?"

"To collect the bassinet for our child to be. I was

pregnant with Atral at the time. My sister had sent a note saying she had a special gift for us. It's tradition in my family to give the mother-to-be a charmed bassinet to promote a healthy baby and good sleep. I never heard from either of them again."

She cradled the tin box with heartache etched in her face. Wolflock gave Mothy a sideways glance and saw his friend doing the same back. The change in her emotional state made them even more cautious of their behaviour and words. Then she opened it to uncover dozens of letters and little trinkets.

"Did you ever receive the gift?"

"No. I don't think many people in that hamlet could write and I received no word from the Hunter's Guild. As far as I know, it never existed."

The acid in her tone made Wolflock realise she believed her husband had run off with her sister. He gestured to the letters, and she pushed the tin towards him. At a cursory glance, it seemed to be a normal sisterly correspondence; swapping recipes, sewing techniques, stories from their childhood and home repair methods. From the details, he gleaned that the woman before him was Finnes Anna, and, after she married, she became Finnes'Anna Slatra. Her sister's name was Maret Anna. Finnes'Anna's husband was Runar Slatra, and his work took him away from the home more often than Finnes'Anna liked. Some of the letters asked to swap spells. Each one had a little sigil in the top right corner. None were dated past the Mabon festival forty years ago.

As he flicked through the letters, maps, sketches, and trinkets, he heard a creak in the hallway next to them. They had an eavesdropper.

"Is your sister magically inclined as well?" he asked, drawing out a map from the tin that marked the significant locations and landmarks between Creast and Mystentine. "Also, could you add the common translations for these names? Otherwise, we will not know where we are."

"We're taking the case?" Mothy gawked. "An impossible to solve forty-year-old case?"

Wolflock shot him a half-cocked grin. "If it's the only way to get to Mystentine, of course we'll take the case."

He thought to tell Mothy later that he would just agree to the terms and see what they could do, but, if they couldn't solve the case, he would just carry on as intended. It wasn't like the old woman could find him again, and the university would protect him by the time she caught up with them. She might even have to wait until the end of Winter to find out what happened and, by then, they would be out of her reach.

"My sister was a witch," she chuckled, gazing off to her right at a painting of a cottage garden. "So was I. The children in town started calling me 'the old sorceress' when I got back after the war ended nine years ago. We inherited magic from our grandmother; Maret used to call my grandmother the same thing."

"You think she's dead? You talk about her as if she's past tense."

"I don't know if she's dead. But she's certainly not family."

"That's a bit cold, don't you think?" Mothy accidentally put his finger through the doily and laid it flat to hide it.

"She left at the time I needed her most. Family doesn't do that," Finnes'Anna snapped.

"And what do you think happened to your husband?" Wolflock pressed, examining the dried flowers from the tin.

"That is for you to find out. I haven't got the slightest idea. His work was messenger stuff for the guild, and he should have been home with the carriage after only a quarter moon."

Wolflock could see her violet eyes burning with rage as she spoke. "Very well. Give us the lion and we'll be on our way."

"I'll need a collateral offering. I can't be giving you such a prize just for deimas," the old woman pondered. "Have any gemstones or jewellery you find important enough to not part with?"

Wolflock touched his left trouser pocket. Himi's beautiful sapphire stayed in there at all times. He wasn't prepared to part with it, though.

"Uhh..."

The crone's eyes flashed over him with a knowing smile. "How about we decide on something if you don't succeed, eh?"

He was sure he could hide Himi's stone by then. "Deal."

The old woman stood up and tended to a kettle on the stovetop. "Dorbi," she called.

The slight movement in the hallway froze and, after a few moments of pretending to arrive, Dorbi came into the kitchen. "Yes, farmor?"

"These fine young gentlemen will take your lion. They've paid handsomely. Go and prepare it for them."

Her face washed with disappointment. "Yes, farmor," she said, then waved to the boys before she left through the back door. "Follow me."

Wolflock and Mothy rose to leave, but the old

woman reached across the small table and took Wolflock's right wrist in an iron grip. Her eyes blazed with a snowstorm of violet and blue, and the room bit so cold that their skin pinched. From her throat, she began a chant.

Vid is vin dinn og sno ji
Sál pín mun ge fa mér gaum.
Bin did med ban og med togi
Ord pitt er skylt ad pet vaum.
Med og med ljoma halfs sins
Bekking Magret Anna og Runar Slatra skalt pú
pekkja.
Settu pinna og snudu honum hreinum
Eg skal vita allt sem pu hefur sed.

Ice trickled up his hand and wound into a band around his wrist. As the spell was complete and the air warmed, a ring of ice hung loosely around Wolflock's wrist. Finnes'Anna clicked her knobbly fingers, and it transmuted into a pewter band with a tiny chain and square-shaped spinning top attached. In the band was a matching hollow where he could place the tiny toy.

"What did you just do?" Wolflock snarled, yanking his hand away and tugging at the band.

"Not again, farmor..." Dorbi groaned.

The old crone cackled, holding her belly, and falling into her chair. "Hoo, hoo! Thought you could slip one by me, did you? Thought you'd take my lion and leave? Might look into it and give up if it's too hard? Going to hide that big old sapphire in your pocket before old Finnes'Anna can get to it? Well, here is some motivation to keep you going, and to be honest next time."

"What did you do?" Wolflock shook the bangle in front of her, then tried to yank it free, but it wouldn't come over his hand.

"That's my insurance. You find out what happened to my sister and husband by the half moon. All you need to do is put the key in the lock and the box of letters, maps and other possessions of mine will all come back to me. Then you can carry on your merry way. If you don't find out what happened, or decide to give up, that bracelet will bring you right back here, where you can give me the gemstone." She interlocked her fingers under her chin and gave him a gummy grin. "Or you can work in the tannery until you pay your debts."

The afternoon sun bounced around the room off all the necklaces and gemstones hanging from the walls. Horror sank into Wolflock's chest.

"You've done this before. These are all your

trophies. And the apprentices outside. Are they willing?"

"Some are willing to learn, others are willing to pay. It makes no difference to me. Now run along. Time is turning. Unless, of course, you want to find other transport. It should only take a week."

Seething, Wolflock balled his fists and snarled at the old woman before storming out of the door Dorbi held for them. Mothy didn't thank the old woman as he followed.

The granddaughter led them to the back shed against the Western Creast wall.

"I... I'm sorry about my farmor. She... I don't have an excuse. I'm just sorry." She disappeared into the shed and came out with a huge mountain lion draped around her shoulders. Wolflock noticed she had also obtained a canvas satchel covered in clumps of short black hair. She saw Wolflock's look of disdain at its size and the daunting task of taking it to Khra. "Let me help you. I have a feeling I know where this is going."

"Thank you. That would be fantastic," Mothy sighed.

Wolflock said nothing.

As they walked back to Khra's cave, Mothy and Dorbi made small talk while Wolflock tried to dig his nail into the pewter band, but the magic stopped him from damaging the soft metal. As they walked on, Dorbi revealed she felt sorry for Khra and would often come out and brush his horse for him. Sometimes they would sit and talk about what was happening in town or about things they'd seen in the forest.

"I always felt like they were sad, you know? Just misunderstood."

"We were there earlier, and they were terrifying. Haven't you ever been scared around them?"

"Scared? No. Not really."

They're both predators. Top of their food chain. They are equals. That's why she's not scared. They recognise that, whether or not they're aware of it, Wolflock thought as they drew nearer. The sun was only an hour from setting and had tucked behind the hill, casting a long shadow over the forest.

"Do you know what he looks like? Is he a demon?"

"Demon? Oh no. I don't think he's human, though. I've only seen him through the vines, and when he's been coming back before dawn. He never stops to chat when he's working, though. He wears a big, broad black hat, coat, and gloves. The sort of thing tourists wear up here when they don't like the sun or the cold. He has two arms and legs, though."

"You don't know how little that narrows it down," Wolflock mumbled darkly.

Dorbi whistled a call out as they entered Khra's clearing. "Hae, hae, Khra. Merry meet. I have your lion."

A loud shuffling of movement came through the vines, and the red eye seemed to glow. "Thank you," came the shrill, throaty voice again. The extra high notes told Wolflock they were pleased to see Dorbi. Or perhaps it was the lion.

"I was going to bring it to you, but it's helping these boys, too. Farmor has played her game with them, so please drive your best for them."

"I always... do my best... for you." Khra made a strange purring noise and the willow roots bristled, but didn't part. "Come to the gate... with your belongings... Sunset."

The same chill of fear prickled over the boys as they felt Khra's attention turn to them. They thanked Dorbi as they backed away and ran for the Mermaid's Paddle. They didn't stop running until they reached the front door.

As they burst through the oceanic stained-glass doors, they crashed into two burly sailors.

"Found 'em Cap'in," Grogen shouted over his shoulder.

Captain Blutro looked fraught with anxiety as he paced back and forth in a clearing in the bar. Grogen and Hognut grasped the boys by their shoulders and steered them to the captain.

"Thank the gods! Are you hurt? Where have you been?"

"I- What is going on? Captain? We're fine." Wolflock frowned, gently pushing Grogen's hands off his shoulders. The sweat from running made his shirt sticky and uncomfortable under the big sailor's shovel-like hands.

"Chosin, we've found them." The captain shouted to the innkeeper, who ran out from behind the bar quivering like a leaf in the wind.

"It's never happened before. Not in my inn. No, sir. Not never."

"It's still never happened, man. It's fine. They're fine," Captain Blutro said as he patted the innkeeper's back, but it also seemed to be to reassuring himself. "Don't be alarmed," he looked to the boys, "but someone has been through your room."

"What?" Mothy blinked. Wolflock stayed silent, waiting for the captain's direction.

"You may be able to make either heads or tails of it, Wolflock. Follow me."

The boys and Chosin followed the captain to their room on the landing stairs. He gestured for Chosin to give him the master key and then he opened the door.

The neat and homely room he had expected to see had been obliterated in a storm of feathers, straw and shattered wood. Someone had tipped Wolflock's belongings all over the floor and they scattered his clothes about. Every single piece was shaken and crumpled. Both of their beds had not only been upturned, but torn to shreds. The feathers had come from someone tearing apart the pillows and the straw from them hacking apart the mattresses. Wolflock noticed that the thin, metal jug of water by the bedside table had been thrown in anger at the window, cracking it like a spider web.

He stood, bewildered, in the middle of the room. Had someone been after Mothy and him? Were they drunk from the festival? Had they come into the wrong room and sought a brawl? Were they looking for something?

"We'll clean this up, Chosin. We'll see what we can do about anything that got broken," Mothy offered, but Chosin shook his head.

"No, mi'lad. I should be offering you reimbursement for anything that was damaged. I pride myself on the safety of my patrons and this... this just isn't right."

"Nonsense!" Mothy pressed. "I feel horrible that you'll need to mend those mattresses and the window!"

"Nonsense," Wolflock mumbled to himself, stepping across his trunk as the scene burned itself into his memory.

He carefully picked up his clothing and looked over his possessions, finding none of them had been damaged beyond the initial search. The intruder had been looking for something. Was it Lord Therym or one of his son's friends? No. His son didn't really have any friends.

"When did you find all this?" Wolflock asked, touching his mattress. The tears along it reached all the way through. They had sliced the fibres with something sharp, and yet they zigzagged through the fabric. One of the puncture marks had three gashes coming out from its centre. Was this the work of the curvy knife from the ship?

"This morning when I did my rounds for housekeeping. I rushed back down 'ere and started sending notes out to the local sailors to see if anyone had seen ya, but I got caught up when Stra came to look for you. I said I didn't know where ya all were, and he said he'd wait for you at the carriage. He seemed quite upset that you weren't around. He got a bit testy when I told him I didn't know where you two had ended up after the festivities. Then I got the crew to look all over for yas."

"Where were you both?" Captain Blutro asked sternly.

"Dr Qwan took us to breakfast after we realised we'd slept in and Stra had left without us. Then we found someone with a carriage to take us to Mystentine. We're meant to go and meet them now, so we came back for our bags and maybe a snack for the road," Mothy answered, pulling a face as he looked around. "We'd best clean all this up. We need to get going."

Without checking to see if anything had been stolen, Wolflock pulled his journal out of his vest pocket and began writing everything he saw down. He wrote and sketched every detail he thought would be important, as well as the description of the particular slash mark.

Captain Blutro turned to the innkeeper. "Chosin, go and prepare water and food for their trip to Mystentine. I'll help them clean up here."

Chosin knew better than to argue with the captain and closed the door behind him as he left. Mothy began picking up feathers and scraps, helping Wolflock find his things after he closed his journal. The blonde boy at least had the wherewithal to keep his bag on him at all times.

He travelled light, whereas Wolflock had his satchel bag and his trunk of clothes, toiletries and a few trinkets he didn't want to leave with his sister in Plugh.

"It'll be ok, Lockie. Nothing seems to have been stolen or too badly damaged. I feel bad for Chosin though," Mothy sighed and scooped up more feathers.

"I'm not bothered about that, Mothy. It's just..." he glanced at Captain Blutro and decided he didn't want to talk about feeling unprepared for situations such as these. Mothy's belongings had been safe, yet they scattered his about. He didn't know who had been in here, or why, and the feeling choked him. "It's fine. We'll put everything back and move on. We'll be out of here in... what? An hour? Maybe two at the most."

He felt like an idiot. There were clues, he knew were there. He knew there were people who had likely seen the culprit. He just didn't know how to find any of them.

The captain saw his demeanour change and put a firm hand on his shoulder. "Finish putting away your things and take a quick bath. You've both gone through a lot in the last couple of days and you don't want to start the last leg of your travels feeling gross. My room has two tubs. I'll get them filled while you both finish up here."

Wolflock couldn't summon any more words. He

managed to nod and nothing else. It took him time to scrutinise everything he picked up. He couldn't see anything different. He wondered if there were tools or objects better than his magnifying glass that he could use at Mystentine to help him solve these mysteries.

If there aren't any... well... I'll just have to make them. He clenched his jaw as determination drummed through him.

As they finished cleaning up the room, Chosin returned and tried to give back the ink he had been given in exchange for their room, but Wolflock flatly refused.

"It's good quality ink! Take it and be grateful," he snapped as he realised someone had stepped on one of his shirts, leaving a shoe print. It wasn't clear enough to make out a pattern, but he angrily drew the shape of it in his journal, shoved the shirt on top of his neatly folded ones, and slammed his trunk shut.

Wolflock took a fresh change of clothes up to Captain Blutro's top room suite. He and Mothy both had time to soak in floral hot water and use all the captain's fancy soaps. Chosin even brought them ice-apple cider, old cheeses and dates to snack on while they cleaned up. The moment of rest and quiet as they waited for the sun to set left them sleepy.

During his bath, he tried to remove the pewter

bangle again before a thought struck him. They may have been after his journal, he realised. He was leaving the protective eye of the Silver Ice Hair crew for good. He had to have an insurance. Just like Finnes'Anna.

He splashed out of the tub and pulled a dressing gown over his wet body before he snatched up writing materials from the desk in the captain's room, and began frantically scribbling letters to Myna and his father. He didn't care if they made sense. They would figure them out. But someone had to know all the details he'd discovered. One day, the threads would come together but if anything happened to him or his journal the mysteries may never be solved.

After an hour the captain knocked on the door and re-entered his room, seemingly pleased to see the boys were in better spirits.

"Grogen, Hognut and I are going to take you to your carriage," Captain Blutro announced in his usual tone that showed he would not be taking any objections.

Wolflock agreed without a fight. They were about to depart from a town where someone had been seeking to rob them, possibly kill them, to a carriage being pulled by a sunlight adverse horse and rider of gargantuan proportions. All to get to a destroyed hamlet to find out how an old ice crone's sister had run off with her husband. He wasn't in the mood to fight the captain.

"Are you sure you won't rest up? I'm happy to post these letters, but please. I'm sure Blutro is happy to share his suite for one night," Chosin begged as the sailors gathered Wolflock's luggage and the provisions prepared.

"Not to worry, Chosin. We've got to be off. We'll stay longer next time." Mothy smiled as he hoisted his bag over his shoulder.

"Please, at least stay for dinner!" Chosin implored.

"I'm afraid we cannot. It's imperative that we move onwards with all due haste-"

"Then let me at least pack your coffers with food! You've been good guests-"

We haven't even been here a night... Wolflock rolled his eyes.

"-So let me send you both off with plenty of grub before you go. I packed a bunch of non-perishables, but we have a lovely pie on for supper tonight. I'll just go get it wrapped."

"Really, Chosin, it's fine-"

"Only if you insist!" Mothy grinned and elbowed Wolflock in the side.

Moments later, the biggest Silver Ice Hair crew members escorted them to the Northern gate of Creast, shrouded by the smell of a delicious blackberry pie. Wolflock felt a sense of satisfaction when the three large men stopped in their tracks.

Before them stood the enormous black carriage with a horse at the front. At seventeen hands high, he expected to see a hairy hoofed highland draught horse, but even he was shocked to see the slim frame of a racehorse.

"What is Houl's name..." Hognut coughed ash out of his pipe.

"This... is your transport?" Captain Blutro baulked.

"Certainly is. Khra has promised to get us to Mystentine in five days. Given we can solve this old lady's problem on the way." Wolflock nodded as if it were completely normal.

"O' course yeh are..." Hognut shook his head and his shoulders shook. After a moment he burst out in wheezy laughter, clapped Wolflock on the shoulder blade and buckled over.

Wolflock watched the taciturn, monosyllabic crewman cackled like a mad man and it made him chuckle too. He had never been sure if Hognut didn't reveal all the shenanigans he caught them in the middle of because he didn't believe what they were saying, or if he found them entertaining. Regardless, he laughed along with the old crewman in appreciation for his compliance.

Everyone stared in wonderment until he stopped and moved to their provisions and luggage. The crew loaded Wolflock's trunk and the food into the storage areas at the back of the carriage and secured them. Mothy hugged each of them, not wanting to let go.

"If you need anything at all, just send word. Come land or sea, we'll be there," Grogen promised as he squeezed the blonde boy, eyeing the dark transport with the utmost concern. Wolflock grinned as Mothy turned purple from the bear hug, only to look away when he heard the horse make a gutteral snort.

"We're ready when you are, Khra." Wolflock walked around the front to see their driver, glancing back at the Silver Ice Hair crew.

His duster jacket made his vast frame even larger. His chin rested on his chest and his broad-brimmed hat hung over his face. Greasy, thick strands of hair clumped down his shoulders, reflecting the moonlight. He loosely held the hefty reins that Wolflock could see weren't attached to the horse in any way that could control them. Black clothes covered their driver from the tips of his fingers and toes all the way to the top of his head. Wolflock couldn't even tell what nationality he was, as his accent was so strange. He didn't move.

Wolflock jumped as the horse neighed a high call, and he rushed to the door of the carriage. Grogen pulled him into a tearful bearhug, sniffling into his damp hair.

"I'll write to yeh. I will. You get ta tha' there university and wait for my letters, yeh hear?"

"I hear, I hear. I'll let you know when we arrive. Merry part, Grogen."

"And merry meet again, lad. Merry meet again."

Captain Blutro cleared his throat. "Can I have a moment, gents?"

Grogen and Hognut nodded and made their way back to the gate.

Wolflock waited for the captain to tell him off or give cryptic advice, but he just stood there. After a few moments, his eyes brimmed with tears. "I don't want to let you make this journey alone."

"Captain, listen. You can't- wait. What?" That was far too clear to come from his Captain. He'd expected some kind of restraining mentoring order. Not pleading.

"You have been a right pain in my rear for the past few months and I should be glad to be rid of you, Wolflock, but I'm afraid for you. It was bad enough thinking someone on the ship wanted to hurt you. Seeing how much danger you attract to yourself and those around you... I can't, in good faith, let you go without offering you alternatives."

"Do you have a cart?" replied Wolflock dryly in order to break some of the emotional tension. He caught Mothy's expression of hope and felt a pang of guilt for dragging his friend through this journey. But they had to get there. They had delayed enough and they'd fought so hard to get where they were. He couldn't turn around now. He couldn't.

"Work on the Silver Ice Hair with us for a few months. We'll do a half round and you'll both be back by mid Spring." Captain Blutro's face creased with deep concern.

"Captain... Thank you, but I must decline. We will be safe. I... I chose this path. You'll always be the captain of the Silver Ice Hair, my first home away from home. But I need to be the captain of my life. Mothy and I are going to study at Mystentine University. That's our plan and we're sticking to it. Come fire or flood, we'll get through anything together. Thank you for everything," Wolflock sighed, feeling his ship loving heart crumble with his words. "Merry part, Captain."

Captain Blutro shook his hand before pulling him into another tight hug. "Merry meet again, Wolflock."

Aujin purred on Blutro's shoulder and wiggled

about until a long thread of shining silver hair caught on Wolflock's shirt.

They parted, and Wolflock stepped into the carriage with Mothy. It smelled musty and old, but it wasn't chilly like the air outside. Wolflock knocked on the front wall and the horse started trotting. The boys watched out of the window as the brightly lit town of Creast and the crew of the Silver Ice Hair vanished behind the trees.

CHAPTER 5

Long Lost Words

Wolflock sat against the front wall of the carriage while Mothy sat at the back, fiddling with the loose threads on the once ruby red velvet seats. The fabric, worn down to its base, smelled like musty curtains.

"Are there any pillows or blankets?" Mothy asked as Wolflock tampered with the little windows to see if they opened enough to let fresh air flow through.

"Check under your seat. There is normally something there for overnight travel." Wolflock pushed open the tiny awning window. They could hear the clop of the horse's hooves, but not a sound from the driver.

Cool night air leaked into the carriage and Mothy found old woollen blankets to wrap around them. They ate some of their leftovers from breakfast and a small slice of pie in relative silence, exploring the compartment wherever they could reach. Wolflock soon grew tired of holding the bone match Dr Qwan had given him and looked for something to keep it safe.

"Mothy, I bet you I can find something that has never been touched in this carriage," he smirked.

Mothy looked around and, not being able to find what Wolflock was talking about, gave a shrug. "Go on then. Surprise me."

Wolflock pressed in a panel to his right, and it clicked, releasing a little platform that had a set of six long-stemmed wine glasses fastened in a velvet lined bracket. In the centre of the bracket was a symbol shaped like five Vs, with a single line running through them and a dash coming off the first and fifth one. "That's interesting."

"That's brilliant! Are there more panels like that?"

"Seeing that this place revealed these types of glasses and not the tumblers I was expecting, yes." Wolflock drew out one glass and wedged it between the shoes he had removed and set the match in it. "These glasses are normally reserved for bubbly drinks and sabbat celebrations. You know? When adults indulge in drinking alcohol."

"They drank wine from bowls or straight from the bottle where I came from. Hazzim never touched any alcohol. I've never seen glasses like that before." Mothy took one out and examined it all over, looking through it to see how the images around him were distorted.

"This carriage likely had very wealthy clientele riding in it. How did it end up in such disrepair?"

"Lockie, I think we've had enough mysteries for one day. Let's finish these buns and get some shuteye, aye?"

The boys were so tired after the events of the day. All their running around, the anxiety of being burgled, and the lull of the hot baths meant that Wolflock couldn't help but wordlessly acknowledge that it was time to sleep. Mothy used his bag as a pillow, as usual, and Wolflock doubled up two cushions squashed to pancakes from use. Before resting his head, he checked over the pillows, their cases and the blankets, finding, on the material, stains from various perfumes, oils, a few burn marks and something that looked like long dried blood. They hadn't had more cleaning than a rinse and a shake, but the night was too cold to forgo the blankets.

Wolflock moved to turn out the match, but stopped. His hand hovered above the wine glass when he caught Mothy's eye. The trepidation of being left in the dark had hit them both. They couldn't see, but a predator could. Mothy had cocooned himself in his blanket with only his face poking out. His blue eyes watched, but he said nothing.

Wolflock pinched the match out.

The moment darkness engulfed them in the carriage, a shrill shriek emanated around them, shaking them to their bones. He scrambled to clutch the match and struck it against the window, bringing the carriage back into a grey-white light. As the light drove out the darkness, Wolflock could have sworn he saw shadows slither into the corners of the compartment. The sight left him with a sick feeling in his gut.

"Uhh... light on?" he joked nervously as he saw Mothy peek out from under the blanket.

"Light on."

They both curled up tight under their blankets, and it took them a good half hour to relax again from their fright. Mothy fell asleep faster than Wolflock, but, as he drifted off, he saw the trees moving past in a feverish blur. The last thought he had before falling asleep was that the carriage must be going quite fast indeed.

~~*~*~*~*

When Wolflock woke, the stationary carriage felt

strange. He opened his eyes and the morning sun greeted him by trying to battle the grime frosted windows. Its pale light made his match irrelevant, so he pinched it out and pocketed it. From his few days working on the Silver Ice Hair, the unclear windows irritated him. Grogen had told him that part of the joy passengers had on their journey was being able to see the power of nature up close, but in safety, so it was important to keep their windows clean.

He saw no difference here. Taking up his bi carbonate and peppermint oil tooth powder, he mixed it with a little water on his handkerchief and wiped off the internal grime as best he could. He saw the exterior windows had been cleaned, either by weather or elbow, but it was a rough job, as if the cleaner didn't bother about the corners or tight edges.

When he finished, he felt satisfied. It may have been the shadows from the window dirt that caused them to be so spooked last night. Now they could rest more easily. He also gave the curtains a bit of a shake to see what state they were in and freshen up the space. The dust that flew off them made Mothy cough, waking him up as he fell off his seat.

"Is this room service? I can't afford it," he muttered between coughs and trying to curl up again under his blanket like a turtle.

"Rise and shine, sleepy friend. We have a big day planned. We have maps to check and data to collect."

"I'll sit back and watch you, then?"

The pewter bangle clinked against the window as Wolflock refastened the faded black curtain. "Only if you want to be left alone on your journey to Mystentine."

Mothy lifted the blanket enough to eye Wolflock. "What do you mean?"

"I'm the one wearing this thing, yes? So, only the tin box and I will be taken back to Creast. You'll be left here to finish your journey with Khra..." Wolflock's voice faded as he realised his joke about Mothy being scared would actually leave him in possible peril.

Mothy threw a shoe at the back of his head. "Don't be daft. You'll solve the case. You always solve the case. Now, you look over your notes and maps. I'll get breakfast ready. It may be bugs and berries, though."

"Check under the carriage. Sometimes cooking equipment is stored there. Watch out though. It is normally cast iron and quite heavy."

Wolflock stepped down and took a breath of fresh air. The daylight warmed his face, filling him with energy. Khra had stopped in a clearing with a stone fountain that had fresh water glittering as it spouted out of a statue's prayer hands. For a moment Wolflock felt disorientated.

They were on the left side of the road. If they were heading North, they should have been on the right. He looked at the clumps of snow and fresh grass for wheel and hoof tracks, only to see they formed a semi-circle off the stone road. Khra had driven the carriage all the way around so that the door faced the road.

Strange... Why didn't he just pull over to the side? Why go to the effort of turning the carriage all the way around?

"You don't know your way around a kitchen-"

"Incorrect. I didn't know my way around a kitchen. I feel fairly comfortable with it now." Wolflock said as he ran his hand over the straps keeping his trunk strapped to the back.

"-but you know where the cooking equipment is on an old wagon?" Mothy followed him out and pulled a large black pan and frame from where Wolflock had suggested.

"My family has raised horses and made vehicles for most of Grothener and the surrounding countries for generations. Father made sure the fastest horses were always commissioned for emergency services and we've been building carriages like this for a long time. I always liked to sneak into the engineers' offices and add extra bits and pieces to their designs. In some of the Guard carts, there is a secret compartment for books and trinkets. Myna told them it was for snacks, but I'm the one who put it in there and I made it big enough for five journals or a handful of items."

Mothy set up the breakfast fire and patted himself down for a match. "Can I use yours?"

"The bone one doesn't light anything on fire, remember? I'll see if Khra has anything."

Wolflock walked around the carriage to find their driver when he spotted Khra and his horse under a black canvas awning held up by short tent poles stuck into the ground, pulled from a reel low on the opposite side of the carriage from the door.

"Good morning, Khra. Was your drive pleasant? Would you have any matches on you?"

He bent down to see the large driver with his broad hat over his face and his hands resting on his stomach. The monstrous horse laid beside him with its legs tucked in and its neck curled around its driver's head. It eyed him with a large dark eye that sat too far forward for a horse. For a moment, he thought Khra was asleep, but then:

"Someone... may have left... matches... in the seat." Khra spoke in long low rattly sighs, but Wolflock couldn't see his chest move in the shadow.

Perturbed, Wolflock walked around the canopy to the front of the carriage, stopping only to pat the horse's neck. It flicked its ear towards him, but, otherwise, didn't move. The black horse's fur felt sleek under his palm, as if it had been recently brushed. He realised Dorbi must have been fond enough of the horse and groomed it before they began their journey. He hadn't seen anything in Khra's possessions that showed that level of care.

He plucked his hand away and closed his fist, staring with wide eyes at the wall that was the horse's neck. It felt ice cold. It felt ice cold, as though it were living, breathing stone; he could see it breathing slowly, slower than even a horse in deep sleep. Wolflock kept his distance as he walked around it and hoisted himself up into the driver's seat. The seat lid lifted to reveal a dark blue jacket and other possessions.

He checked the pockets of the jacket and found a packet of matches in an ancient, cardboard packet. The paper had yellowed, and the white tips of the brittle wood had chipped. He supposed they were too old to be useful and left them in the pocket. The collar of the jacket had the same golden insignia as the glasses they had found last night. In another pocket was a small notebook, bookmarked with a card for an inn called Eksynmatkal Hengähd. The card was so old and had likely been used in the diary so often that it had worn its edges down to fluff.

As Wolflock closed the seat, a glint of light caught his eye. A hand sized hook hung out of the top edge of the carriage. He gave it a yank to see how firmly it was attached and it stretched out a foot and a half before retracting. It hung directly over where Khra sat. Did it keep him upright while he was sleeping? Did the horse do the driving? From the harnesses attached to the carriage, it looked that way. Was he so sick he needed to hook this into his shirt? Wolflock made a mental note to see how Khra interacted with this hook later on.

Still thinking, he took the card and the journal to Mothy, who had tried to make a fire by rubbing two sticks together.

"Here. Matches. Try to use them sparingly. I don't know if we'll find a place to get anymore before we get to Mystentine City." Wolflock tossed the matches to Mothy.

As the blonde boy made a fire, Wolflock piled over the newfound diary and maps Finnes'Anna had given them. It took him a moment to find the fountain on the map, as it was much further along the road than he expected. Different tracks lead off to neighbouring towns, forests, rivers and sacred sites, but the ones along to the road to Mystentine and mentioned in the letters

Finnes'Anna had provided them were the Eksynmatkal Hengähd inn, Restöfundsjúkum hamlet and the Hunter's Guild, marked as Veidimenn Deild on the map. The inn's common translation was "Lost Traveller's Respite" and it seemed the closest out of all the necessary locations.

"If we could get to this location," he pointed to the map at a fountain marked on the road, "by today, we should be able to get to the inn by tomorrow morning. Or very near to it, at least."

"Is there anything nearby that would be fun to see?" Mothy asked, tasting the broth he was using to rehydrate some salted chicken.

"We can always look at that fountain. Apparently, there are several of them along the way. There are very few streams that cross the road near here and, to make sure people and animals travelled safely, the temple of storms blessed these fountains to always make clean water."

"That's amazing," Mothy said.

"Mmm... storms rejuvenate the enchantment."

"When did you find all this out?"

"Some of it's in these letters. Finnes'Anna mentions to her sister to remember to bring about a storm once in a while. She says that the ones closest to

Creast are fine. She takes care of those." Wolflock flicked open the diary from the blue jacket and read it while Mothy finished making breakfast.

As he read, he realised the author filled it with reports from local townsfolk asking for aid from the hunters' guild. Records of strange creatures, missing livestock, and injured farmers filled the book, as well as their outcomes and the guild members who tended to the problem.

Sidumpus the 2nd of Col'uc Gaia, 4th year of Queen Circia

Client goat herder Holtog Grimish reports six goats missing every full moon for two months. Blood trails lead into the darkest parts of the forest before vanishing. Sent the son to investigate. Hasn't returned. Suspected wolves, but we'll see.

Result: Some kind of ghostly monster that lives in dolls and anything that vaguely resembles a human. The more terror it creates, the stronger it gets and the better-quality vessel it needs. Went from a little straw dolly to a stuffed toy, a puppet and then a shop mannequin. Originated from a merchant at E.H. Volseggir and apprentices burned it down. Only minor injuries sustained.

Leyndarmal Ad Aftan

Relimpus the 14th of Xissyli Sor, 5th year of Queen Circia

Client seamstress Ulga Trolovska reports three girls in the village of Hulsa have gone missing after washing by the river. Blyrkjun says the witch told him it was a Nokken. Going to try his iron needle and riddle idea first before taking a sword to it.

Result: It worked! The witch was right. All the people going to wash at the river now know to sing a riddle song as they go down, but the needle weakened him enough to maybe not even need that. Nokken was last seen playing some kind of fiddle but hasn't interacted with anyone since. Going to E.H. to celebrate.

Leyndarmal Ad Aftan

Ferimpus the 20th of Xissyli Sor, 6th year of Queen Circia

Client priest of light Auldos Huxfich reports draugr rising from the burial site. Volseggir went to slay them. Blyrkjun and I had to rescue him as he defended the priest. The witch said the stolen treasures had to be returned to their grave. Spent a good day and night battling draugr while the priest tried to remember which graves he took them from.

Result: we can turn draugr into wood chips and their splinters will still try to retrieve what they were buried with. Also, don't rely on Volseggir to give records on priests and temples. It was a Troston priest taking over an old abandoned light church. Thank goodness for the witch and her remedies. I'll need a rest at the E.H. and a good dose of whatever she made that helped us through that ordeal.

Leyndarmal Ad Aftan

Quintampus the 10th of Ha'ling Felst, 7th year of Queen Circia

Clients Finnes and Maret Anna report a demon trying to steal townsfolk. Got one. Believed to be a demon of obsession as it's only targeting strong young men. Apparently, one of the young girls had an unrequited fondness that she let consume her. The witches have warded the village, but no one can leave. Sent word by crowl. I was starting to get worried they'd forgotten about us. Haven't seen them at E.H. for months.

Result: I told Blyrkjun I wouldn't hunt a demon at night, and he refused to come with me. Volseggir came along with five of the apprentices. Three slain, one maimed, one fled. Demon destroyed. I'd never seen a woman sob more over a monster than that one did today. She begged us to capture her, but nothing would have stopped it. They're not human anymore when they hit that point. I tried to explain that, but she seemed furious at us. I'd never wanted those ancient spells to revivify a creature more. It's done though.

Leyndarmal Ad Aftan

Relimpus the 28th of Ha'ling Felst, 7th year of Queen Circia

Client Finnes Anna reported a troll she couldn't be bothered to deal with. Women. I'll sort it out. No need for help with just a troll.

Result: Wasn't a troll. Was a demon. Bloody women. Showed me that a demon can revert back to human. She'd been baking this one for a long time just to show me the moment they healed. Volseggir followed us. Killed the demon. Finnes said she needed to get away for a while. She didn't want to deal with the guild anymore. Couldn't make her stay for anything. Not even telling her about my office at the Eksyn.

Leyndarmal Ad Aftan

Sollempus the 26th of Alung unt te Gaia, 7th year

of Queen Circia

Client Finnes Anna reported loneliness. Met her in Creast.

Result: Married. Don't know how I'm going to break this to Volseggir. He's been made guild leader. Blyrkjun didn't want the position. I'll keep doing my work, but I'll try to travel less. Maybe we can start our own tavern. That'll be a grand time.

Leyndarmal Ad Aftan

Sollempus the 18th of Frum'ling St'sol, 9th year of Queen Circia

Client rancher Agana Vorscht reports draugr slaughtering cattle and draining their blood. Doesn't sound like draugr. Blyrkjun sent out. I said don't engage, just collect information. Volseggir said my wife is making me soft. Told Blyrkjun to wipe them out.

Result: Blyrkjun injured. Nothing helping. Brought him to Maret Anna. She has a remedy that seems to be working.

Leyndarmal Ad Aftan

Sollempus the 18th of St'lung Luna, 9th year of Queen Circia

I still haven't told him. I don't want to put him in

danger. He's the best hunter we have. He's like a brother to me. Maybe I can change him. I have to get back into the library.

Wolflock frowned at the last entry. It wasn't like any of the others. It was written in the same hand, but he wasn't sure it was meant to be there. After six more pages, the final entry said:

Lucimpus the 1st of Eolas Revari, 9th year of Queen Circia

Client witch Maret Anna reports bubak in Restöfundsjúkum hamlet. Killed three goats and a farmer. Best clear this out before I marry her. Finnes'Anna will be mad, but she'll be happy again, eventually. It's been a hard secret to keep. I'll bring any books I can find on it to the E.H. for us to plan.

Result: Set the trap with Blyrkjun's contribution to the Samhain parade. Everything is going according to plan.

He flicked to the back of the book, but many of the pages had been torn out. The only piece remaining was a paragraph that said:

Sidumpus the 2nd of Col'uc Gaia, 4th year of Queen Circia

Not knowing what this was or how to destroy it made me delve into the library under the guild hall. I had to go through an old storage room, trapdoor, and then a haunting hallway, but I made it. Take a better torch next time. There are old oil lanterns, but they aren't filled. No one has been down there for generations. Old Master Drask said the best training is on the field, but it doesn't hurt to know something from books. As Keeper of Secrets, I'll only share this with the new guild master Drask picks. Still looking for what this creature was.

He felt certain that this was Runar's diary. It seemed he had run off with Finnes'Anna's sister, but that didn't explain where they had gone or why his coat and carriage ended up in the hands of the eeriest driver he'd ever encountered. And what did "Leyndarmal Ad Aftan " mean? Was it a send-off? Or some prayer?

Mothy passed him a bowl of stew and Wolflock slipped the inn card inside the book.

"Good read?"

"Informative. It looks as if Runar did run off with Maret. In his last entry he mentions marrying her and Finnes'Anna being displeased. There are pages from the back missing, and he mentions a place by the initials E and H a few times, as well as a place he calls the Eksyn. I believe he's talking about the Eksynmatkal Hengähd Inn. It's a night's travel from here."

"We're losing a day without discovering anything, then?"

Wolflock sighed. "We can't drag the carriage ourselves and it's too far to walk. We're going to have to rely on our driver to get us there."

"How far did we travel last night? Show me the map," Mothy sidled up next to Wolflock to look over the old paper together.

"Creast is here," Wolflock pointed, "And we're here. You can see the fountain mark."

"How far is that? It looks like miles."

"It is. About sixty."

"Sixty!" Mothy spat out his mouthful of soup.

"I was surprised too. Don't look a magical horse in the mouth, though."

"I don't know what that means, but I am very curious to see the inside of this horse's mouth!" Mothy craned his neck to see the horse and driver through the gap under the carriage.

"You can tell how old and healthy a horse is by their teeth. If you find a magical horse, or you're given the services of a horse, it's rude to be critical of it and look in its mouth. I never thought I'd be giving you an etiquette lesson, Mothy."

"It's obviously a phrase used for princes and the like," he chuckled, still trying to see under the carriage. "How far away is this inn?"

"About twenty-five, thirty miles."

"That's only half the distance, though. We'll be way past there by the time morning comes."

"I was thinking we'd ask Khra to stop for a moment so we could have a look around."

Mothy dropped his voice. "Do you think that's safe?"

"It's all we can do. Otherwise, we wait there until morning and lose half a day... night's travel."

"I suppose it's an inn. It will have a keeper and maybe some patrons to chat with. We might get a lot of information out of them. The innkeeper is likely to know lots."

"That's a good point. I'll organise Khra when he wakes up this evening. I'd rather not disturb him or his horse again."

They explored the clearing, keeping away from the carriage for the rest of the day, reading the letters and new book until they committed them to memory. The boys made a game of following the patches of sunlight that scattered warmth between the clouds, partly to move around and partly because, whenever they fell under any kind of shadow, they both felt a sense that someone was watching them. They avoided the treeline and jumped at every sound the forest made at them. The gekkering of a fox, the squeal of a rabbit, the shriek of a bird; all of them sounded too human and in distress. After a few hours, they sat back down to make lunch and make up songs to keep their spirits high.

"Remember the old sigils for protection on the Silver Ice Hair?" Mothy asked, as he served cheese and marmalade sandwiches for lunch.

"I have them drawn in my journal. Why?"

Mothy leaned in, dropping his voice. "Want to put them on the inside of the carriage?"

Wolflock nodded, his eyes growing wide as he realised Mothy's genius. "Absolutely. They're sleeping right next to the carriage, though. Do you want to make noise so they can't hear what we're doing, or shall I?"

"You do the noise. I'll copy them out of your book. You're good at talking forever and I'm good with my hands."

"Done."

They finished lunch and packed up the cooking

equipment, tucking it back under the carriage before boarding again. Wolflock paced in the little space they had, talking loudly about the horses he'd seen and how prestigious they were, as well as unique carriage designs and all of their engineering properties. Mothy used the end of a knife Chosin had packed for them to carve protection sigils on each window frame, on the floor, the ceiling, and the door. It took all afternoon, but they felt much safer when it was finished.

Mothy held his hand over each of them and said a prayer for protection in native Chalhl, the language of mid to Northern Chalongesh. As he finished, Wolflock heard the canopy Khra and the horse were under retract. He saw the sun had set behind the trees, leaving the sky pillowed with grey clouds that had pink and ginger linings, and the enormous beast rose. Its back reached the height of the windows, and it seemed to ripple with power. He saw Khra's hat, but he couldn't see the driver. Only the horse. He must have been leaning on the horse, and the boys could hear an odd, wooden clacking sound as he walked. The front of the carriage dipped as he got into his seat.

"I'll ask him about stopping at the inn." Wolflock stepped out and found their driver in exactly the same position he had been in last night. Hat tipped far down over his face and reins draped in his black-gloved hands. The horse seemed to help him adjust by nuzzling his leg. "Uhh... excuse me, Driver Khra?"

The horse froze and kept still, its huge eye staring right at him. Khra didn't move.

"We would like to stop for a short time at the Eksynmatkal Hengähd Inn tonight. Are you able to service this request?"

"I... can stop... down the lane... You will walk... to the... inn," Khra wheezed in his throaty, yet shrill voice.

"Why can't you take us to the inn directly?"

"Lane... too small... for me... to turn."

"Ah. That's reasonable. It's not a long lane, then?

"Not long..." Khra paused for a moment. "Keep a... light. Light... keeps you safe."

"Thank you. I hope we don't need that to be helpful."

Khra waited as Wolflock stood there, wondering what the light would keep them safe from. After a few moments, the driver rumbled, "Get in."

The dark-haired boy flinched and shot back into the carriage, throwing himself into the safety of his seat as the carriage started off. It jerked forward so fast it threw Wolflock into the opposite seat. He scrambled back to his own seat and lit the match, dropping it into the wineglass. The carriage turned, and the horse cantered back onto the road.

CHAPTER 6

Going Inn the Dark

Through the opened window, they heard the rumble of hooves and wheels. The speed was so fast neither of them could stomach looking at any of the letters, maps, or notes. They couldn't even manage a conversation. They felt like they were in a terrible dream.

"I'm glad we missed this last night," Mothy groaned. Wolflock could only nod.

Every corner they swerved around pushed them back and forth along their seats, and they held on for dear life. White knuckled and wide eyed, they tried looking around inside the carriage, but they just felt nauseous. They tried looking out, but the smudge of trees racing by them did the same. The only solution was to close their eyes and hope it ended soon.

Wolflock didn't remember feeling sleepy, let alone falling asleep, but he remembered waking with a start from a nightmare that slipped past him. Mothy jerked awake with a gasp only a few seconds later.

"We've stopped?"

"Seems so."

"Fantastic. I was looking forward to getting to this inn. Maybe they'll have a nice pot pie or some fresh bread. I think living off that seed bread for a year has made me relish soft ground grain breads." Mothy stretched his shoulders as he got to his feet.

Wolflock took up the wineglass with the bone match in it, lifting it to shine the grey light across Khra, who looked as if he hadn't moved throughout their terrifying journey.

"Wait here for us. We shouldn't be more than an hour or so."

Khra nodded as the horse shifted enough to rock the carriage and remained silent.

"Good conversation. See you soon, Khra." Mothy waved as he backed up towards an open gate leading up a hill through overgrown woods.

It wasn't much of a gate. Just a thick, roughly cut log stretched between two X brackets on either side of the dirt lane. Beside them hung an old sign with one person giving another a bowl of food and the Shirth letters for "Eksynmatkal Hengähd". Deep trenches showed where carriages had frequently rolled up and down the hill to the inn.

Wolflock kept the wine glass high to shine as much light as possible. The overcast sky left them in total darkness except for the flickering light they had. Mothy wrapped his arm through Wolflock's as they trudged up over the hard dirt.

"It must be a pretty far lane to the inn. Why would it be so far back?" Mothy whispered.

A small whoosh of wind like someone running with a cape made them both jump, stumbling over the wheel trench.

"What was that?"

Wolflock's heart drummed in his chest, and his jaw clenched. He felt Mothy shiver beside him. He had to be brave for his friend. If he showed he was frightened, there was no hope.

"Just the wind from an animal running from us. We must have startled it. Let's keep going."

He pulled Mothy along the road, expecting, at any moment, to hear people and music, but nothing besides the icy wind tearing through the trees came to them. The light cast shadows through the trees, creating spectres that Wolflock tried to avoid seeing.

They weren't equipped to handle ghosts. They had no salt or iron or amulets. No priestly words off the top of his head came to keep them safe. It took all the courage he could muster to not just turn tail and run back to the carriage. But he pressed on.

"How much further do you think it is?" Mothy whispered again.

Wolflock yelped as a sign creaked overhead, then coughed to mask it. "Ahem. The trees look thinner just over the ridge. It should be there."

The boys continued walking until a twig snapped behind them, and they broke into a sprint to the top of the hill. A large clearing opened before them in a fenced-in field. The wind rustled the grass and a nearby owl let out a long, low 'hoooo'. But, as the clouds split and the moon shone across them, they both breathed a sigh of relief. The evening felt much safer in the light of the moon.

Panting to catch their breath, they looked at one another and burst out laughing, cutting through the nervousness the darkness had laid on them. As they finished their bout of laughter, Wolflock looked around. He saw the inn about thirty feet away, realising why there was no light emanating from it.

The burnt-out shell of the Eksynmatkal Hengähd Inn stood in all its brittle glory before them. Only the old stone chimney remained.

"This wasn't in Runar's notes," Wolflock said slowly, his shoes crunching on blackened charcoal. How were they meant to find out any information now?

"Do you think it was an accident? Kitchen gone wrong? Oil lamp spill?" Mothy began kicking pieces of timber to clear a path through the middle of the inn.

"The kitchen is over there," Wolflock waved his hand to the chimney and the stone benches around it. "This fire was old. You can see by the smoothing and wear on the burnt wood. A lot of the charcoal has been washed off the top, but if we move these planks..." He walked through the rubble and, lifting a half-burnt rafter, he heaved it to the side. "Thank goodness the roof was thatch, otherwise we'd be shifting tiles for days."

"What do your fae eyes see, oh wise one?" Mothy snickered, rolling an armful of planks out of the way.

"That this is strange. This wasn't a multistorey building. We can tell by the shell leftover. It's like a longhouse. The fire must have started somewhere here. This is where the most damage was done, but there is no starting point for this V shaped burn marks inside the building," Wolflock huffed, stepping out of the debris, and sat on an old burnt stump. "Fires spread from a V shaped point and flare out like a triangle."

"How did you know that?" Mothy laughed and stepped out after him.

"I used to burn lots of things so I could tell if Myna was putting my toys in the fire."

Mothy frowned sceptically, "And was she?"

Wolflock sneered. "This is Myna we're talking about. Of course she was."

"Of course she was... Umm.. Lockie?"

"Why have so many pieces not been making any sense?" He wrapped his long, thin fingers through his black hair.

"Lockie, look."

"I got us lumped in this mess because I couldn't tell the old woman was so conniving. I couldn't tell who tore our room to shreds, I can't tell what's wrong with that driver and I couldn't-"

"Lockie!" Mothy clapped in front of his face. "You're possibly sitting on our origin point."

Wolflock leaped to his feet and shone the wine

torch over the stump. He'd never seen a cleaner cut and the entire tree had been charred. As he lifted the light higher, he saw the distinct black V stemming from the tree stump.

"How does someone set fire to a stump and then it catches onto a whole building?" Mothy tilted his head from side to side.

"Because it wasn't just the stump." Wolflock looked out across the building and saw one rafter that looked much larger than the others. "It was the whole tree. Someone set the tree on fire and then cut it so it would fall on the inn. And I bet you it has something to do with Runar's notes. This area is filled with tiny villages and hamlets. Nothing someone would destroy an entire inn for, surely. Runar kept secrets and hid things away, even from the people closest to him. There has to be something else here."

Wolflock walked over the burnt down inn, looking for anything that hadn't been destroyed.

"Lockie? Lockie!" Mothy pointed out into the field next to the inn. Wolflock looked up and saw a post with something blowing in the breeze around it, only visible as the waning full moon lit the field. "I swear that scarecrow wasn't there before."

A chill ran through Wolflock's spine. "Mothy.

Come here to me. We need to go."

"It's just a scarecrow, Lockie. Don't try to spook me now."

Wolflock kept his eyes fixed on the scarecrow. "Mothy. Now. Get over here."

"You're not going to frighten me, Lockie. No way, no, sir."

"Mothy, this isn't a joke. That is a bare field. It's not a crop field."

Mothy tensed. "What are you saying?"

"There shouldn't be a scarecrow in it."

The scarecrow's pumpkin head turned, staring directly at them with a maniacal grin. Wolflock pounced forward, grabbing Mothy's shirt and hauling him around the wreckage towards the lane. The sound of the twigs breaking and straw clipping from the scarecrow monster racing towards them mixed with the night's wind and Wolflock had one thought.

Get back to the carriage.

A black shape leaped over them, and the scarecrow cut through the treeline, leaving deep gashes in the bark of the pine trees. Wolflock pulled Mothy to a stop before the lane, realising they were easy prey. Sticks snapped and leaves shook just inside the treeline wherever they looked.

He didn't know which was worse. Staying in the clearing like a sitting duck or risking being snatched into the foliage like a pigeon in a fox den. Wolflock stepped back, clutching Mothy. He wouldn't let his friend be hurt.

"Lockie, what was that?" Mothy breathed as the wind grew quiet again.

"I don't know."

"How do we get back to Khra?"

"I don't know!"

Panic rose in his throat and his voice cracked, just as sticks on either side of the laneway snapped. From the right-hand side grew long sticks, winding into a jagged archway above them. The boys backed up into the burnt inn as the sticks took shape and the despicably carved pumpkin found its way to the middle of the spider shaped creature.

"Mothy, run!" Wolflock shouted, pushing his friend behind him. Mothy grabbed his wrist and pulled him through after him.

The scarecrow pounced forward, but the burnt floor under them gave out and they both fell through into a dusty basement. Wolflock saw Mothy knock his head on the upper floor as he fell and laid still. The dark-haired boy fell onto his stomach, winding him and sending a nasty shock through to his back. He couldn't breathe and he curled into a ball to protect himself from more falling debris. The room spun, but, once he could draw breath, he scrambled over and saw Mothy's back rising and falling. He was only unconscious. The floor above them creaked, and he heard the creature making low, whining noises, like a baby. At one point he could have sworn it called out "Lockie".

He'd dropped the wine glass holding his match and he could see the match still burning amongst the shattered glass. The flame was dimmed on the cold stone ground.

Please stay lit. Wolflock prayed silently, his eyes darting from the light to the roof above them. Please stay lit.

Just as it died out, the scarecrow above them scurried away, frightened by heavy steps approaching. A deep snarling noise rumbled over them, but, after a few moments, disappeared. What could have been more frightening than that thing?

"Lockie?" Mothy mumbled, opening his eyes in the dim light. "Lockie, what happened?"

Wolflock grasped Mothy's hand, squeezing it as hard as he could. "Thank goodness."

"Were you worried?"

"Worried I'd have to carry your heavy lump of a

head back to the carriage," he snorted. "The floor gave way. Our search hasn't been for naught, though. Something bigger scared off that monster and we've found a secret basement. It looks untouched by the fire."

"The scarecrow? I'm not sure I like Shiriling at night."

Wolflock chuckled in agreement. "Can you stand?"

"Let me try." His friend wobbled to his feet, rubbing sore places over his head and chest. "Am I bleeding? No, it's you. Lockie. Your hand."

Wolflock lifted his right hand to find a deep cut down on the pink side. "I must have fallen on a nail. Let me get my light and make sure it wasn't anything rusty."

The little streams of moonlight that trickled through the burnt holes in the floor above let him find the match with relative ease, and he struck it into full life again.

"Where are we?" Mothy asked, but he gasped as the light touched the edges of the room.

From the stony floor to the battered ceiling were monstrous heads mounted on the walls, racks of weapons, and cabinets filled with sharpened stakes tipped with silver. In the middle of the wide table in the centre of the room lay a map littered with holes from the thin daggers pinning it to the wood. Everything was branded with the symbol of the five Vs with the line through them.

"This must have been why Runar and the other hunters came here so often. Maybe they had this space because they kept the tavern safe." Wolflock looked over the large map and found holes in the locations corresponding to the diary. Someone had stabbed one knife into Restöfundsjúkum hamlet. The last place Runar had logged in his journal.

"This is a pretty scary space. What are all these things?" Mothy picked up a mace and dropped it on his toe as soon as it was free from the rack.

"Weapons for hunting monsters and dangerous animals. The Hunters' Guild in any region keeps the people safe from aberrations and act as stewards of the forest. Like Dorbi in Creast."

"Oh, aye? And what's an aberration?" Mothy drew a sword he struggled to hold up, pretending to swing it like a knight.

"You didn't learn any of this? I thought they taught it everywhere; how to manage relations with fae, spirits, gods and other creatures."

"I may have learned it by other means and names. You never know. Aberration is a big word. You can fit a lot into it."

Wolflock chuckled, searching for books and registers to give him a better idea of what had transpired here. "Aberrations are typically made by magical means. They consume negative energies and, sometimes, are able to take enough to replicate themselves."

"Oh, of course. A simple as that then. Whoops." Mothy swung the sword with too much confidence and it sank into the head of a roaring yeti behind him.

"They're creatures made by magic. Sometimes the magic a wizard or a witch uses, sometimes the magic a being naturally generates. This produces a single focused monster like that scarecrow, and it develops into," Wolflock waved his hand to the ceiling, "whatever that scarecrow thing was."

"So, it didn't start out that way?"

"No. It has incorporated too many human items into itself to have been made like that. It probably started out as a spider looking thing or a spiky plant. Then, as it fed off the negativity around it, it grew stronger. Some of them never make more of themselves, others make a lot."

"Like a disease?"

"Very similar. Just bigger. We could see that, but we can't see a disease."

"What does that one feed off, then?" Mothy picked up a hand axe and nodded approvingly.

"I'm not sure. Fear? Pain? Suffering? Grief? The screams of children? Could be anything." Wolflock laid his hands on the only bookshelf in the entire room. Far dustier than anything in the room, he took out the only book that seemed to be frequently used. It was a binder of legal agreements, contracts and other things the higher guild members had officiated.

"Everything in here is used to kill monsters, then?" Mothy put the axe on his belt and took up a recurve bow and quiver, aiming at the yeti head he had left the sword in.

"No. These things will work just as well on humans, werewolves, vampires, and more peaceful creatures. I even saw some well-crafted iron things to harm fae. This guild was hunting everything."

"Werewolves and vampires are peaceful where you come from? They sure aren't in Chalongesh. I used to hear all kinds of terrible stories about them and what they'd do to people. Some folks from Ulusai'il would pass through with missing bits because of werewolf encounters."

As Wolflock skimmed through the register, he found multiple cases where the same families that had sought the Hunters Guild's assistance would later sue for damage to their properties, injury to family members, and harassment. The guild paid off the patrolling Guard to stay out of their way and had experimental alchemical contracts with local potion brewers. He frowned as he read on, seeing that the guild had many dirty dealings, and, after Runar's disappearance forty years ago, the issues had only increased. Intimidation seemed to be their most effective marketing method.

The last record came from thirty years ago. A baby's naming ceremony had been conducted right where Wolflock stood.

As the Great Mother Pelaia gives soul to our life, we name this child Blandt Oviru in health of heart and mind.

By the strength of the mother, Oviru, Maret'Anna, we lay this blessing of guidance to all things compassionate.

Maret had signed her name separately in a pre-written naming ceremony certificate. Wolflock noticed her surname wasn't Slatra. She had fused her first and second names when she married, but it wasn't Slatra. Had they both changed their names to hide their indiscretions?

By the care of the father, Oviru,... we lay this blessing of longevity to live a life fulfilling.

The edge was burnt off and he couldn't read anymore of the name.

"Lockie? Did I upset you?"

"Huh?" Wolflock blinked out of his thoughts as Mothy touched his shoulder. "Oh. No. Sorry. I think I've found something."

"What is it?"

"Look at this naming certificate. Maret is the mother."

Mothy sighed. "I guess old Finnes'Anna was right then. Her husband ran off with her sister."

"No. No, he didn't. His surname isn't Oviru, and this isn't his handwriting."

"Then why did he say he was going to marry her?"

Wolflock pinched his chin and strained. The words were right there. He married Maret... But he didn't get married to her.

"That's it Mothy! He married her. To her husband. He officiated the wedding! That's why he said Finnes'Anna would be mad. She didn't get to attend her sister's wedding. People always get worked up about silly things like that."

"But then why didn't he come home afterwards? And why hasn't her sister contacted her since?"

"And why did they have to marry in secret? And did the monster that dropped the flaming tree on the inn intend to kill them?" Wolflock exhaled, looking around the room for more clues.

Before he could search for more information, the boards above them creaked again with an even, slow tread, sending trickles of dust and ash cascading to the floor. The boys held their breath. They hoped whatever it was would just pass, but, as they shrank back to the wall, they weren't hopeful.

Then they saw a pair of worn black leather boots as they descended the stairs, bringing down a dark mist. The man of sinew and darkness spotted them and raised a gleaming sword, pointed directly at them.

"And what have we here?" he smirked, and Wolflock couldn't help but see the pointed canines and flash of red eyes.

Rhiannon D. Elton

CHAPTER 7

Hungry for Answers

"Who are you?" Wolflock raised his left hand, preparing to defend himself, while pushing Mothy behind him with his right.

The pale man raised his elbow, supporting his blade as he stepped forward, keeping it at Wolflock's throat height. "I don't think you're in a position to be asking questions, stranger. Who are you, and why are you down here?"

As he stepped into the light of Wolflock's match, he saw the boy stood a few inches shorter than him and his skin was as smooth as porcelain. He held the sword expertly, prowling forward like a lynx. His dark brown hair stayed off his face with tight braids down either side of his head, and his arms were as pale as his shirt. Wolflock initially mistook him for wearing long sleeves until he saw they were rolled up to his elbows. His black trousers sat loose around his upper legs until they tucked into his snug, knee-high boots. He looked like a fencer except that he had a bag on his hip and two knives in each of his boots.

Wolflock eyed the boy. He thought he was a man at first, but his youthful face made him realise he couldn't be older than him or Mothy. "What is that to you? You don't own this land."

"We were looking for the inn," Mothy spoke up. "It wasn't here, and some kind of monster chased us. When we ran across the remains of the building, we fell through the floor."

"Oh, really? And where is this monster now?"

Wolflock hadn't broken eye contact with the stranger. They kept looking at Wolflock's cut hand with their gleaming red eyes and that cold smirk. "They ran away."

"Monsters in these parts don't run away when they start a chase. Or when they catch the scent of blood."

"And are you a monster, vampire?" Wolflock

snorted derisively.

The boy froze. "What are you talking about?" He dropped his sword and Wolflock saw the symbol of the Hunters Guild engraved in it near the hilt.

"Do you not know what you are, or do you have to keep up a façade for the guild you're a part of? I heard they think quite poorly of vampires in Shiriling."

"I thought you said vampires are nice," Mothy hissed over his shoulder.

"I said they could be peaceful. They're just as temperamental as humans."

"So, do we run or rush him?"

"Neither. He's faster and stronger than both of us together."

"I can hear you; you know?"

"He has enhanced hearing too?" Mothy gasped.

"I'm not a vampire!"

"Then why are your eyes red, your skin pale, and your teeth pointed?" Wolflock growled.

"I feel like it's rude to ask someone why their skin is so pale. And for your information, my eyes are not red. You are mistaken. It appears you aren't monsters either, though. They aren't nearly as inquisitive. Who are you, and how did you find this place?"

The boy lowered his sword, but kept it

unsheathed.

"You're part of the Hunters Guild. You should have known about it."

"How did you know I was part of Veidimenn Deild?"

"You're equipped to the teeth for combat and your sword bears the Hunter's Guild insignia." Wolflock emphasised the word teeth.

"Just because I like my meat rare doesn't mean I'm a vampire. I hunt for the guild at night and my eyes are an odd hue, but they certainly aren't red." The boy rolled his eyes and Wolflock saw they weren't red. They were violet. "I see our trust is at an impasse. I'm Blandt."

"Blandt Oviru?" Wolflock blinked. The naming certificate was thirty years old. This boy looked no older than fifteen.

Blandt blinked and shook his head, his sleek eyebrows pinching. "No. Saga. Same as my uncle."

"Volseggir Saga?"

The pale boy's eyes went wide, and he put his hand back on his sword hilt, "How do you-"

"We found this place because we have been sent by Finnes'Anna, the old sorceress of Creast, to find out what happened to her sister and husband. She believes that forty years ago they ran off together, but I have found evidence to the contrary. Runar Slatra married Maret Anna to a man with the surname Oviru. We just found a naming certificate for a child with the same name as you bore thirty years ago."

Wolflock's excitement about the strange pieces of this mystery nearly falling together, yet repelling apart like magnets, made Mothy and Blandt look at one another with dubious stares.

"Maret Anna, you say? She... she's dead."

Wolflock stopped. "How?"

"It... it was this very inn. She came here with me for my naming ceremony, just as the paper says. But it was only seventeen years ago, not thirty."

"You're seventeen?"

"Aye. I am."

"Bit short for seventeen," Wolflock snorted. "You know vampires age at one quarter the rate humans do."

"Again, rude. Don't know why you're like this-"

"You learn to find the good points amongst it," Mothy shrugged.

"-but I'm not a vampire. I can go in sunlight, and I have never killed an innocent person to drink their blood. See? Not a vampire. They're feral and bestial and-"

"So you've killed guilty people to drink their

blood?" Wolflock pressed.

"What? No! I haven't killed any person to drink their blood. Why am I even answering these questions?" Blandt threw up his hands and stormed upstairs into the night.

Wolflock trotted behind him. "In Plugh, we see vampires all the time. They live in an underground city and have a completely symbiotic relationship with the people above. They're not feral at all and they have a strict society that keeps them all in order. I bet you're the best hunter in the entire guild, aren't you?"

"What of it?" Blandt huffed as he stalked to the lane in the direction of their carriage.

"You're faster than the others, aren't you? Stronger too? You have better hearing, better sight. Blood smells good to you, even if you can resist it. Why can you resist it? Were you bitten?"

Mothy followed them out with his arms filled with weapons light enough to carry, looking around with an alert eye.

"You're talking nonsense."

Wolflock prodded him as Mothy joined them beside the black carriage. He wanted to get Blandt riled up. "You could have been bitten as a baby, which is why you're ageing so slowly. How did they let a vampire in the

Hunter's Guild?" Blandt walked as quickly as he could down the lane where their carriage waited. "From what I saw in Runar's diary, Volseggir was a total bigot and a useless hunter-"

Blandt caught Wolflock's throat and pinned him high on the carriage with such speed and force it rattled through his chest.

"Don't," his eyes burned red, "you dare talk about my family, stranger."

Mothy dropped his bundle of weapons and leaped forward, holding an arrow to Blandt's back. "Put him down."

Wolflock grinned. "No claws. Red eyes on emotional upset. Heightened speed and strength. Canines extend with emotional excitation. You can put me down now."

Mothy and Blandt looked befuddled. The pale boy lowered Wolflock and clenched his fists.

"You," Wolflock panted, "are a half vampire. Maret Anna's husband was a full vampire. Likely one who was bitten and had to keep it secret in the guild. There! Mystery solved. Let's get this band off!"

Mothy frowned as Wolflock took up the square pyramid on the end of the chain of his pewter bangle and put it in the corresponding hole.

"Huh? I missed something."

"Runar died trying to trap a bubak, and Maret Anna died when the inn burnt around her. Done and dusted. We can relax the rest of the way to Mystentine," Wolflock turned the shape. He expected it to melt or disintegrate, but it did nothing. "Any second now." He turned it again. And again. And again.

"Should something be happening?" Blandt asked Mothy.

"Not sure. We were told we had to find out what happened to old Finnes'Anna's husband and sister from forty years ago. We've been through diaries, maps, this old carriage. Everything. That's what brought us here. Then we found out it had been burned down and that big scarecrow thing attacked us. Why were you out here?"

"There are a few wolves that have been stealing goats. I wanted to relocate them further away from the roads."

Wolflock tried turning the dial in the opposite direction, snarling at it as the other two continued their conversation.

"Oh. That sounds familiar. I think I've had a few people pass through with the same task. Not for many years, though. Could I see the maps? Maybe I could help. I know these parts better than anyone except Uncle Vol."

"That would be great." Mothy heaved a sigh of relief. "What can we do to repay you?"

"Nothing. I want to find out about why the naming certificate you have has the wrong date and wrong surname for my mother and I. A bit of a vested interest but you seem reasonable enough. If you share your information, I'll share mine. Deal?"

"Deal!" Mothy and Blandt shook hands as if it were a casual day. "Oh. Cold hands."

Wolflock stared wide eyed and nose twitching. He had tried to remove the bangle by putting it between his shoes and pulling. "If that was all it was going to take-"

"No. Not you. I'm sharing my information with him. He's polite. You're a goblin."

"Now who's being rude?"

"Where is the guild? I'm sure you know a faster way than the maps we have." Mothy interjected, ushering them into the compartment.

Blandt followed, but Wolflock stopped to check on Khra and his horse. The driver hadn't moved, but the horse panted, its head lifting and dropping rhythmically.

"Is your horse well, Khra? Did the night startle it?" Wolflock moved to the horse, which looked at him with a red shine to its reflective tapetum. "Were you attacked by the scarecrow thing?"

The horse snorted. Wolflock reached up, knowing what to expect, and stroked her sweaty neck and shoulder. She felt like she'd been bathed in ice water.

"There, girl. You'll be fine. We'll leave now and find a safe clearing to rest up. Stop if you need to rest. Khra, we're heading to the Hunters' Guild. If your horse needs a drink, make sure you stop."

He received no response from the driver, but the horse snorted again. Wolflock grew up around horses and he could tell a noise of appreciation when he heard one. Checking on the horse calmed down his nerves enough to get into the compartment with Blandt and Mothy.

He sat next to Mothy and leaned in the seat's corner and the wall of the carriage, growing tired from the excitement of the evening. Blandt spent his time pouring over the maps and Mothy chewed a long strip of dried ginger as he tried to not be sick until he fell asleep curled into a ball on his half of the seat.

"Tell me about your uncle," Wolflock said, unable to drift into slumber.

"After my mother died, he took me in. Him and aunt Retta. I remember them fighting a lot until Aunt Retta suffered from a mind affliction. Now she just wanders around as if she's a shell. Uncle looks after her, makes all her meals and does all the paperwork for the guild."

"Is there much?"

"No. Mostly purchasing and answering requests. He sends me out to take care of things."

"Isn't that dangerous for a small seventeen-year-old?"

"I'm more dangerous than most creatures out there. I don't know how, but I seem to always make it through fine. Whenever I've been at my worst, I black out and then wake up a few hours later by a campfire and a fresh deer or pheasant. I sometimes think I'm a better hunter in my sleep." He chuckled and pointed to the map in his hand. "This is where we find Aunt Retta when she's having an episode."

Wolflock looked at where he was pointing. "That's the road to Restöfundsjúkum, isn't it?"

Blandt nodded.

"What's there now?"

"It's an old hamlet. There're a few farmers, potters, weavers. One farmer has an extra shed he rents out to artists and travellers. It's a pretty little place. I didn't know my mother used to live there. What do you think you'll find?"

"I'm hoping to find the answers to Runar's

disappearance. It's the last entry in his book. Are the people from forty years ago still living there?"

"A couple. Some died, some moved on." Blandt looked away, his cheeks colouring ever so slightly.

Wolflock scrutinised his tense posture. He knew more about that than he was letting on. "Why are they moving on?"

Blandt sighed. "They are frightened. Before my aunt lost her mind, she would take me out on hunting missions to learn about the monsters and creatures we hunted. She taught me about keeping the balance in nature, reading the signs, and the weather. I thought I remembered fewer monsters being around then. My uncle tells me the people wanting our help need proof that the creature is gone, so I have to bring back a head or a limb. Something to show the monster has been neutralised."

"But there has been an increase?"

Blandt nodded. Then shook his head. "I mean, I don't know. It just feels like that. The people focused on it too much and moved to places they thought were safer."

"Hard to focus on anything else when your life is on the line," Wolflock muttered darkly.

"It won't matter soon."

"Why is that?"

"Mystentine University is trying to buy the Veidimenn Deild. It's only a matter of time before they're able to win my uncle over."

"Ah." Wolflock understood. "They're buying the guild so they can increase their branch of studies into the creatures that lurk along the roads and nearby areas. I also believe the guild has a magnificent library they'd find quite valuable."

He waited for Blandt's response. At first the boy continued to look over the map, but after a moment, he blinked in alarm and looked up. "How do you-"

"Runar's diary. He mentions stumbling across it and keeping it a secret from Volseggir for fear of him destroying it."

Blandt bit his lower lip and relaxed back across the seat. "Wouldn't be the first time. Volseggir says that reading tears families apart. Children who read leave to go and study places. Adults who read keep dreaming of something more. Something they'll never get."

"We'll that's ludicrous. Reading is what saved countless lives for Runar in this diary. It's what is going to help Mothy and I get to Mystentine University and not magicked back to Creast. It's what keeps your land in balance. How else do we pass on knowledge?"

"Volseggir says speaking is a lost art."

"And what if, like Runar, they die before they can pass the message they need to on? Or they forget, like your aunt?"

"I'm not disagreeing with you. I enjoy reading. Mostly maps and stories. Uncle Vol is going to not like hearing anything about a library. That's all."

"After looking through Runar's journal, I had no inclination to reveal this hidden trove of books to Volseggir, if that's what you're getting at. I just want to find any information on Maret and Runar. After that, we'll leave."

"Excellent. We can stop for food and a rest. I'll show you both the guild. We'll look up the name Oviru and then head to Restöfundsjúkum to see if the old cottage has any answers."

"I'm normally the one to make the plans." Wolflock raised a dark eyebrow as he wrapped himself up in a blanket, feeling sleep finally washing over him.

Blandt shrugged. "I'm the only one allowed to do anything at the guild. None of the others are trained enough, yet."

"How many are there?" Wolflock yawned.

"There's eight students. Uncle Vol calls them apprentices, but they aren't on the job, so they're really students. He doesn't like the word students because it makes him think of the university meddling..."

Blandt spoke on and on about the guild, which was just what Wolflock needed to fall into a light sleep.

His nightmares that evening were more vivid. He stood on a blood red carpet with all the people he hated in Plugh yelling incoherently at him. The more he tried to argue back, the more they grew, until they stood like giants around him. He panicked, feeling trapped. He looked around for any escape, but there were no gaps between their monstrous, mangled forms. Then, in between the cracks of their arms and legs, twigs grew that wound into a spider-like creature above him. A pumpkin face turned down with a sickening grin and launched at him.

Wolflock woke with a start, feeling the grey autumn sun help him escape the dream. He took a moment to remember where he was and looked around the carriage. It was empty besides him. He stretched and stepped out of the carriage, seeing they had pulled over in that semi-circle fashion on the left-hand side of the road. The sun's position told him it was mid-morning, and the charred smell of breakfast said Mothy had been awake for at least an hour.

He spotted his friend twenty feet away, aiming the

bow he'd found at a tree.

"That's it. Much better. Elbow up, hold your stomach tight. And, release," Blandt yawned, sitting in the shade of pine branches caked with snow.

"Merry morning," Wolflock called out as he scavenged a plate of scrambled eggs from the pan. Mothy had set their breakfast fire up right next to the clean water fountain. It wasn't as overflowing as the previous one, but it didn't have terrible signs of degradation. Who had tended to it if Maret had been missing for forty years?

"Good morning, Lockie! Blandt's teaching me how to shoot this bow. How'd you sleep?"

Wolflock walked over with his plate, taking a few mouthfuls before speaking. He saw Brandt had taken one of the carriage blankets and had it wrapped around him like a hooded cloak.

"I had terrible dreams. Other than that, surprisingly restful, considering I didn't lie down."

"Me too. The dreams I mean. I felt so helpless yesterday. I thought learning how to shoot might help us in case the rest of the journey is perilous."

"Good thinking. Whatever soothes your nerves." Wolflock watched him take a few wobbly shots as he pondered what would soothe his own nerves. He spotted Khra and the horse lying beside the carriage under their canopy and knew what would help.

He took his plate back, gave it a scrape, and began searching the carriage for any tools for horse care. Eventually, he found a maintenance container on the back of the wagon with an old hook for scraping out the hooves, a pair of rusty pliers and a brush. The handles felt dry and brittle, but they would do.

"Khra, I know Dorbi brushed your horse before we left, but I would like to check her health, if I may."

The horse looked up at him with its brown eye. Khra said nothing.

"I'll take that as an affirmative." Wolflock crawled under the canopy.

The horse wagged its head this way and that, but he touched its cold, flat forehead. His hand looked tiny on the gigantic beast.

"Shh. Shh. All is well. All is well. You're safe," he purred softly, soothing the mare. "You're a magnificent girl. Yes, you are. I just want to make sure you're fine after last night's shock."

His words seemed to confuse the horse, but his voice and body language made her stop fidgeting. He brushed her over, feeling relaxed by the methodical procedure and the splendid results. She had no lice or fleas, and she didn't seem to have an undercoat, which struck him as odd because the weather was so cold.

"You're an odd girl, aren't you? I'd say you were part kelpie, but we're not near any water. Can you speak? Blandt is half witch, so you may be able to talk to me."

The horse snorted, moving her head under her driver's hat and nuzzling him with her lips.

"No? I guess he's not witch enough. We'll definitely have a witch or two closer to Mystentine." After he finished brushing her down, he picked up the pliers and hook. "Is it fine by you if I clean your hooves?"

"That's fine." Khra grumbled under his hat. "My hands... aren't good for... that."

"Sorry to wake you, Khra."

"You didn't..."

Wolflock started with the front hooves, clearing out what looked like years of gunk, grit, and mud. The huge hooves were pointed into dangerously sharp edges to their front, but someone had still put a round shoe on. One nail held the iron on. The hoof had grown around it, holding it in place like a mould.

The state of it horrified Wolflock, who used the pliers to remove it and check for infections. There were none, and the hoof itself was the hardest he'd ever trimmed, but he managed to bring it back to a reasonable state. What made him feel even more troubled was that these hooves matched the strange ones at the shed in Creast that had blocked the river and contained evidence of slavers they hadn't found .

"How long have you lived near Creast for?" Wolflock asked casually, even though his heart beat in his throat.

"Five and ten... Winters..."

"Are you friends with anyone in town?"

"Dor...bi."

"Anyone else?"

Khra stayed silent for a long moment as Wolflock moved to the back legs. His mare behaved well.

"No."

"Do you do business with many people in town?"

"No. The town... doesn't like me... Only those... who pass through."

"Ah. Like traders?"

"Yes..."

"Did you do business at the lumber mill?"

"Yes..."

"Before or after the shed collapsed into the river?"

"After."

Wolflock stopped. He wasn't expecting an honest answer. "What did you transport?"

"A trailer... joined to my carriage. It smelled like...

poison and death... Dirty blood."

"Who hired you for that job?"

"I don't ask for names... I don't... care. They smelled like... poison flowers."

"Lots of flowers are poisonous. That doesn't really narrow it down," Wolflock answered dryly.

"Foreign flowers. From a hot... wet... land... You have some, too."

Wolflock frowned. "Purple ones?"

Khra fell silent again for a moment. "I don't know what... that is..."

Wolflock put down the hook and pliers to search through his notebook. He found the dried purple herb he'd found on the Silver Ice Hair. "Did it look like this?"

"It smelled... like that... yes. More... refined."

Wolflock wondered if it was the purple powder from the Dominia Mendis Impertio, the Lady Mind Master. How could it have gotten onto the ship, though?

"Your horse travels at extraordinary speeds. Why did you charge us so little? Why a mountain lion?"

"That's... my business..."

"Well, if we make it to Mystentine city with time to spare, I'm going to pay for your horse to get proper shoes. You can't leave them on for so long. She's a strong mare, but she deserves better than that. You'll need custom ones, and I can afford to get them made for you. We might get the stable hand at the guild to shoe her temporarily until we can get a master crafter in the city."

Khra stayed silent, but the horse arched her neck back and nudged his foot with her nose. Wolflock smiled and stroked her forehead again. He was becoming accustomed to her cold skin and oddly set eyes. Perhaps it was like chickens learning to be around a dog and vice versa. She turned her head away when she didn't want any more petting, and Wolflock returned to her last shoe.

Using the unfamiliar tool caused him to slip with the hook and reopened the gash on his hand. He pressed the bleeding wound into his black trousers so it wouldn't stain his white shirt, but he heard a terrible panting from the horse.

Her huge red eye bulged out of her head, and her nostrils flared as she sucked in the air around her, gasping for the smell. But it was her open, drooling, long fanged mouth that chilled him. Those huge white teeth, long and sharp, extended like blades ready to strike. Wolflock scrambled back out from under the canopy and the mare did the same in the opposite direction. He tumbled to his feet while she tore free from the canopy, breaking one of its sides and screaming. Wolflock saw streams of smoke seeping from her mane and flanks. She eyed him with a feral ferocity and dug her hooves into the gras, tearing away from him and into the treeline.

Mothy and Blandt heard the disturbance and leaped to action. Mothy ran to Wolflock, but Blandt caught the mare as she entered the shadows.

"Lockie! Lockie, what happened? Are you hurt?"

Wolflock cupped his bleeding hand, watching as Blandt stroked the mare's face, soothing her anxiety after a few moments.

"Wow. He's pretty good with her. Who'd have thought, eh?"

The dark-haired boy grimaced with disappointment, looking away. Mothy took his injured hand and began tending to it from the emergency pouch he'd received from Dr Qwan.

"It's not deep, but we have to keep it clean. What spooked the horse, Lockie?"

Wolflock winced as Mothy dabbed his hand with a few drops of antiseptic alcohol.

"I did. I cut my hand and... Well... She responded unfavourably."

"Oh. So it wasn't the thing in the trees?"

"Huh?"

"I've been seeing something black and... capey. It's been following us since the inn. It's been circling the camp all morning. That's why I wanted to learn to shoot. I thought I might be able to frighten it off."

Wolflock looked to their driver, still laying under the canopy, then to the horse and half vampire. His eyes scanned the forest, and he could have sworn he saw it, too. A black shape flitting between the trees.

"We are surrounded by predators... All we can do is hide. Or run."

Rhiannon D. Elton

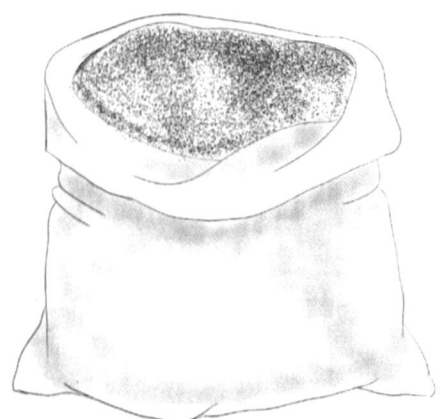

CHAPTER 8

Veidimenn Deild

O r," Mothy said with a blatant firmness, "we can be extra friendly so they know we're good and they will be our friends." Wolflock yelped as Mothy squeezed his hand. "I know you're stressed. I am too. There are too many things around here that are so dangerous. We have friends though. Khra hasn't eaten us yet and his horse ran away from you. That's a good sign, right?"

"I suppose so."

"You're just rattled. Come sit in the carriage. At least it's warded."

Mothy steered Wolflock into the compartment and

closed the door with a snap. They sat down in their seats and, at the same time, heaved a sigh, relaxing their shoulders. Inside, the carriage felt safe. The cleaned windows let in the lovely warm sunlight and the protected room kept it like a plush greenhouse.

"Warding the carriage-"

"Was the best idea we've had so far on this trip," Wolflock finished Mothy's sentence, and they broke out into laughter.

"How are we going to survive university?"

Wolflock wiped his eyes, leaning back into the corner of the seat and the wall. "By the tips of our wits."

"And the charm of our tongues," Mothy added.

"And by the luck the gods left behind."

The urge between them to clink teacups or tankards lingered, but they didn't have anything on them. A silent promise to complete their pledge when they next had a drink in hand filled the air between them.

They relieved the pressure of the day by talking about what they thought Mystentine University would be like, the classes they'd take, and the people they'd meet. The thoughts of the future brought them hope and a renewed energy. In the mid-afternoon, they took a nap in the sun and woke to the cool, dusky air.

"Can you smell that?" Wolflock took a deep breath,

tasting the humidity.

"The impending doom night-time brings on this road?" Mothy chuckled, stretching awake.

"It's going to snow."

"Well, if any horse can get through it, it's yours." Blandt opened the door and sat next to Wolflock.

Unlike the night prior, Wolflock didn't relinquish his seat. He kept his leg on the seat, bending his knee only a little to give Blandt room to sit down. The half vampire sat down and brought his knee up, pressing against Wolflock's as they battled for the seat.

The snow fell as the pink sunset cast shadows between the trees and snowflakes. Khra's horse had no issue tearing through the snow and ice over the road. Her hooves cut through the ground, ripping the ground up and propelling them forward at tremendous speed. Occasionally, between the conversation that Blandt encouraged, Wolflock would glance out of the window. The black figure made of cloth and shadow flashed between the trees, keeping pace with them. He had to tell himself that it was just the shadows cast by his new wineglass lantern. Nothing more. Though, Mothy's glances at the windows made him think his friend saw the same thing.

Blandt, instead, appeared bright and chatty, telling them about the eight apprentices when Volseggir brought them to the guild and how their skills made the guild feel more like home.

"Tultra came from a great smithy that learned everything from the old fae smiths who established Mystentine. They asked us for help with a group of tree spirits who were upset with their logging practices. I moved most of them out, but I had to take one to Volseggir as proof. And then there's Groalani. She is crazy about horses. She's going to love Khra's horse. I find her sleeping in the stables most nights. There are only a couple of horses left and they're pretty old now, but good for a quick journey. She came from the biggest dairy farm in the province. At first, we thought some unseelie were curdling milk, but then it turned deadly. Trolls came down out of the woods and burned the stead to the ground."

"Did trolls do that to the inn as well?" Wolflock grumbled as Blandt's stories woke him up again.

"That was before my time. You'd have to look at Volseggir's records if he still has them."

"He's not good at records?" Mothy asked.

"He hates paperwork. And books. And anyone asking questions. Whenever I wanted to follow up with anyone we'd helped in the past, he'd say he couldn't be bothered writing the case down, or he only has the name and creature involved. He didn't even give the new recruits their symbols."

"Cymbals? Like a musical instrument?" Mothy asked, making Wolflock chuckle.

"No, no. See, we all are meant to have our own identifying symbol that we use like an insignia. It's a variation of the guild symbol. This is mine." He drew a tree made of jagged lines on the window and breathed fog on it.

"That is fascinating." Wolflock took out his book and drew it down.

"Give me your book. I'll write them down. There are also symbols for what action needs to be taken in places. You'll see this one in caves that are safe, this one for people to sell skins to and this one for weapons and armour. Then you have emotional ones like this. I taught the apprentices this one. It means don't touch. Then we've got magical, dangerous, avenge and revenge-"

"Avenge?"

"Mmhmm." Blandt nodded, scribbling the symbols down, "Sometimes a villager will ask for a creature to be killed to avenge a lost loved one or a destroyed home. It's not common, but it's a binding oath for anyone who takes it. There are stories for all of these."

"You'd best tell us all about them then," Mothy yawned. "You've got a lovely voice for stories. What was your first hunt like?"

Wolflock squinted at Mothy before closing his eyes. Blandt kept talking, causing the boys to doze off, only waking every couple of hours to interject with a word or two to keep him rolling. Blandt yawned as the black sky turned grey with another overcast day ahead. The land around them wore a soft blanket of snow, which was beginning to glitter under the pale light. Khra turned a corner, and the carriage went up a dirt drive, past a huge single-story longhouse with more rooms jutting off of it. It looked ancient. Old grey logs, like bones smoothed with time, made up the majority of the guild building, patched with moss and daub.

The carriage rounded into the covering beside the stables and stopped, letting the three of them out. As they came around the back of the carriage, they stopped on seeing a young girl with braided brown hair standing frozen, with her hands clasped over her mouth. She pointed at the giant horse and brought her hand back to her mouth in a silent squeal.

"Happy birthday, Groalo," Blandt chuckled. "They're only here for a little while, so enjoy her while she's here."

"She... she... I can..." the girl stammered breathlessly. She let out a high-pitched shriek of delight and ran to Khra's horse, brush at the ready.

As expected, Khra didn't move, and the girl didn't even notice the driver. The horse stood still in her cart collar and let the young girl begin a thorough grooming.

"She has peculiarly shaped hooves that need re-shoeing before we leave. You have a smithy?" Wolflock walked up beside her as she examined how the harness of the carriage fit around the horse.

"This is strange. How do you keep the horse in the carriage? Huh? Oh. Yes. Tultra will get the shoes made. Goodness, you're right! She does have strange hooves. Did you file them? Are you expecting her to go into battle?" The girl ran her hand the full length down the horse's front leg and lifted it to examine underneath. "You need to change her shoes more often. You've just recently taken them off, no?"

"She's not mine. I assure you if she were, I'd have her shod far more frequently. With the amount of travel I expect she does, she'd need it. I believe," he shot a glance at Khra, who still hadn't moved, "the carriage gets more attention than she does, and it still isn't that much."

The horse snorted in affirmation, craning her neck around to see them with her strange eyes. Wolflock could see they were quite a bright red, even in the shadow of the awning over them. He could have sworn they had been black when they met.

"She... Uh... gets spooked around blood and I'm not sure what she normally eats, but don't try to feed her. She'll find food when she's ready. Also, don't look her in the mouth."

"Never look a gift horse in the mouth," Groalani chuckled, measuring the gigantic hooves with her hands. "And no sunlight, yes? She hasn't been bitten by a vampire, has she?"

The three boys tensed. No one in the guild suspected Blandt of being half vampire or half witch, and Wolflock didn't know how they'd respond to the strangeness of a creature they normally hunt being under their hospitality.

"I... I doubt it. She seems to just have very delicate, thin skin. She may also have a layer of fat across her from her breeding. That's why she feels cold."

"I was about to say! She is freezing but not shivering. I've never seen a foreign horse before." Groalani seemed convinced of their lie and enamoured by the magnificent beast.

"Ah yes. Typical for South Grothener warhorses. She's decommissioned, I believe."

The mare blinked at him, flapping her lips around her sharp teeth. She bent down to examine the girl and, for a moment Wolflock thought she was going to bite her. But, instead, she collected her braid in those prehensile lips and played with it, making the girl giggle.

"If you get hungry, you find me first, you hear?" Wolflock warned the horse. "Send Khra and we'll find whatever you need, but don't bother this girl about it, aye?"

The mare snorted again, her eyes blinking slowly in a relaxed way. Wolflock was partially satisfied, but he intended on making sure he returned later and had a good chat with Khra about what he should feed his horse to keep her safe.

"Come along," Blandt waved at them with a yawn. "I'll show you the grounds while the others have breakfast. We won't be held up with questions and kids ogling you. Oh, and tell them you're potential new recruits. We'll say I rescued you from that scarecrow."

"Or that you came just in time to see us fend it off, which is why we were good candidates for the hunter's guild," Wolflock insisted.

"Mmm... No. Mine is more believable."

Blandt walked them around the main paddock, saying that the guild land went on for miles in each direction, but they kept the recruits and training to a smaller area so they could maintain it.

"There are sigil stones that keep out all the worst monsters. None of them can cross the threshold or fences of the land. I've seen them try, and it looks like they run into a wall of water."

"That's a powerful ward. How do you come across it, being half vampire?" Wolflock asked as he sketched the sigil design into his notebook.

"If you keep talking like that, I'll bite you and show you just how little a vampire I am."

"I don't doubt you're only a little vampire. I wonder if your mother knew who she was marrying... And did she know about you? Surely there would have been signs. Did you know you only get a half vampire when a human and vampire-"

"And where do you do your training?" Mothy cut in.

Blandt showed them the obstacle course, weapons training courts and field of magic. The field was literally that. An empty grass field. Wolflock didn't know why Blandt seemed so proud of it until he showed them that it had deep craters when explosive spells had triggered.

"Mother always said that learning how to defend yourself against magic and men was even more lifesaving than learning to defend against the creatures we hunted. She always had a way to soothe a beast or distract them, but people were different, she said." Blandt leaned on the fence leading into the blast-ridden field, violet eyes with crimson flecks dreamy with nostalgia under the shadow of his hood.

Mothy smiled, leaning next to him, experiencing the same dreamy look.

Wolflock froze. Blandt's mother Maret was meant to have died in the fire at his naming ceremony. How did he have memories of her training him in the field? Had he lied? Was this something he'd forgotten?

"Of course, my lessons with Uncle Vol were much more lethal. I never left the training grounds without a cut that needed stitches, or bruises that felt like broken bones. He said never to trust anyone. He used to do these exercises when we had more guild members, where the one who fought the hardest won. Volseggir said it was a lesson in stepping on others to reach the top, and we needed to learn that lesson early, so we didn't let pity destroy us. When the old members left, he left me in charge of that lesson for the new recruits."

"Did you agree with the training?" Mothy asked.

"Yes, and no. I think you need to test your mettle against stronger foes, but you don't need to destroy them to use them as a stepping stone. You don't get higher by defeating people with less power than you. You only get higher by learning from those that are better and more experienced than you."

They stayed in silent agreement for a while as Wolflock thought of a way to bring the conversation back to

Blandt's mother.

"Did your mother agree with your uncle's teachings?"

"Sort of. She taught me a lot about nature and how it was our job to keep the land in balance, but she also had me fight him over and over again, even when I was sick. In the daytime, at my worst, when I was hungry, when I was too full, I thought I'd burst. At random moments, she'd wake me up and get me to train. I think she was scared Volseggir didn't do a thorough enough job."

"How old were you when your training finished?" Wolflock probed, trying to keep his voice disinterested, so he didn't alert Blandt to his underlying intentions.

"Hmm... good question. Mother's hair was all grey, and she's just gotten a nasty wound on her upper arm from a ghoul that caught her off guard. She'd been at the graveyard at Restöfundsjúkum, and I caught it before it could cause any more grief. That would have been three years ago... Hmm... twenty-seven. But... that makes no sense." Blandt frowned. "Listen, I'm not good with maths. And you've got me exhausted. I'll show you the longhouse and then I have to get some rest."

Blandt continued to look pensive as he counted on his fingers the timeline of events he could remember, consistently counting over seventeen years. They found a stuffy, smoky warmth in the longhouse. A pit of embers stretched through the middle of the building with a wrought iron frame over it for the cooking pots and roasting boar. Two of the apprentices argued over how much spice they had left and which meat to apply it to, while another pair wrestled with wooden shields in the far corner. There couldn't have been more than six and seven of them.

"The storage room from the diary should be through here. This was the old Secret Keeper's room until she left. Retta? What are you doing in here?"

Blandt opened the door to see an old, grubby lady with a crooked nose and a thick, black wool shawl wrapped around her shoulders turn to stare at them through a curtain of dark grey hair. Her dull eyes looked at them without recognition and her hand clasped around a small bag of sunflower seeds.

"Wolflock, Mothy, this is my Aunt Retta. Want me to help you with those?" He took her under the elbow and led her out of the room. "You two have a pry around. I'll have a nap out here. Let me know if you find it so I can get in later tonight."

Retta let out a low moan, clicking her tongue at Blandt as he led her out. Wolflock closed the door behind them, and the boys began moving boxes until they uncovered a small trapdoor in the corner. It had an old box filled with containers of a white powder Wolflock dipped his finger into and made a face.

"Disgusting. Ascorbic acid."

"Acid? Is it going to burn off my tongue?" Mothy brushed his tongue down with his hands.

"No. It's dried from citrus fruits. It's meant to be good for you, but it tastes foul. Our governess fed me a dose of this twice a day for years when citrus was out of season. She said it was going to stop me from getting the flu."

"Did it?" Mothy tugged the trapdoor up and leaned it against the wooden wall.

"If it did, I wouldn't admit it. Are you ready?"

"Have you got your light?"

They both looked down the dark hole. Small stone hand holds jutted out of the wall, into the black depths. Wolflock lit the bone match, tucked it into his breast pocket buttonhole, and began climbing down. The darkness looked like the climb was about a hundred feet, but it was really only twelve. A six-foot high, two-foot-wide tunnel threatened to squeeze them into nothingness, but never followed through as they held their breath walking down it. Wolflock ran his hand along the ceiling, feeling the rough carved stone for any openings. None.

"Whoever built this didn't put an air vent in this part.

If they knew how to build basements at all, we should find something further along."

They turned left and Wolflock's match cast its grey light into an expansive room. Mothy shook a few of the oil lanterns, finding they had oil in them, and lit them up as well as the main pillar of sconces. The light cast around the room revealed a huge square hall with stone shelves lining the edges of the room, and eight stone archways supporting the high ceiling.

"Are we under the stables?" Mothy asked, looking up for any trace of sunlight leaking through.

"That far corner is close to it, but I think we're under the place where they graze the old horses. Look for any kind of logs, journals, registers; that sort of thing. Also, keep an eye out for any books on witches, bubaks and vampires. We know Runar stopped using this diary when they went to trap a bubak at Maret's hamlet. We're also looking for pages that could have been torn out of his journal."

"That could have been tucked into any book here..." Mothy rolled his eyes. "Also, these are all in Shirth. I can't read Shirth."

"They aren't all in Shirth. These are in old Puinteylien. And look! This one is even in Chalhl. Try to find what you can. Maybe even just open them and see if any pages fall out."

They looked for hours, and, although Wolflock was impressed by the enormous collection of information the Hunters' Guild had stored here, he found very little in the way of usable information.

The bangle on his arm felt cold. It had been growing colder every day. Whenever he finished looking through a shelf, he put the square spinning top in the dial and turned it, hoping it would give him a clue.

After four hours, he growled in frustration, tapping his forehead on the shelf in front of him. He scrunched up his face and thought hard, focusing on his mental web.

Runar had loved Finnes'Anna and married her forty-two years ago, moving to Creast. As the Secret Keeper of the Hunters' Guild, he used the library to aid his knowledge of how to better deal with the monsters and beasts that threatened the land. He officiated Maret Anna's wedding to a man by the name of Oviru forty years ago, then, in the same entry, mentioned hunting a bubak. He was never seen or heard from again.

Maret and Mr Oviru had a son named Blandt thirty years ago. On that night, someone had both cut down and set fire to the tree outside the Eksynmatkal Hengähd Inn. The Hunters' Guild held that space as a private area, reserved for them, so, logically, only other Hunters' Guild members would know about an event, such as a naming ceremony, happening.

Wolflock felt a chill, thinking that someone Maret and Mr Oviru trusted would have betrayed them and the entire guild so terribly.

"Mothy, if you find any records on punishments being laid out for guild members for misconduct, keep that aside, too."

"I'm sure they have a Shirth ABCs here somewhere," Mothy laughed to himself as he flopped more books around, looking for loose pages.

Wolflock returned to the web in his mind by placing his forehead back on the shelf. If Blandt was the child of Maret and Mr Oviru, and he was a half vampire, it would make sense for him to look so young and remember more years than people would expect, but it didn't answer the question of why he thought he was only seventeen. Or, why he had memories of his mother when he believed her, and his father, died in the Eksynmatkal Hengähd fire at his naming ceremony.

Also, without knowing more about the local monsters and types of aberrations, he couldn't rule out ones that were capable of taking down a tree with some kind of fiery weapon, but the timing was too perfect.

Volseggir was the leader of the Hunter's Guild and possibly resembled a troll more than a man, given his dislike for books and for keeping useful data. His disdain for harmony between the creatures of the land and its people made Wolflock instantly dislike him. He knew from Runar's diary that Volseggir preferred to kill on sight. Was he so uneducated on the very creatures he hunted that he mistook Maret's child for a human? Wolflock didn't put it past him.

Loose threads flew about his face. The land was in a state of decay; the people were leaving. Prominent families died because of the guild's incompetence, and they took on the orphaned.

Blandt had said it was the children no one wanted. But, they came from skilled families and had prime land. Why would no one want them? They all seemed healthy. How did the guild end up with them?

Wolflock opened his eyes in the grey light of his match, looking through the open shelf into the centre of the room. A pair of glowing violet eyes stared back at him just on the other side.

"Ah!" He shouted, leaping back. He fumbled the match and dropped it on the stone floor. In the next instant, he plucked it back up and looked through the shelves. A dark figure slouched in the centre of the room. "Mothy!"

A pitter patter of shoeless feet came down the tunnel

and one of the young boys popped through. "Ms Retta, where have you gotten to? What have you found?"

Moments later, a second one appeared. They both stood with their jaws open, gazing around the room.

"Wolflock? Are you done in here? Oh? What's this now? How did you three get down here?" Blandt followed them through the tunnel, looking bedraggled.

"Blandt, what is this place?" one boy asked.

Wolflock and Mothy came out from the shelves, waiting for his response.

"Well... Umm... This is called a library, boys. You can't tell anyone else. It has to be our secret. Uncle Volseggir wouldn't approve of all this. You know he doesn't like us reading."

"So we can't come down here?"

"No, no. We just have to keep it a secret for now. I have a plan and then we'll be able to read all these books whenever we want. Now, run upstairs and let me know if Volseggir comes looking for me." Blandt ruffled their hair and sent the pair away with Retta. Then he turned to Wolflock and Mothy. "I think I may have remembered something. I had a dream just now. It seemed real, though, as if it wasn't a dream. I remember my mother and Volseggir fighting. We had a plan. We were sending letters to the university to tell them how to get rid of the monsters on the land they wanted so they could buy it before Volseggir could. He's been trying to buy up the entire region between Mystentine and Creast. We had a plan to stop him."

"How do you know it wasn't just a dream?" Mothy asked. Wolflock pinched his chin in thought.

"Because in my dream, mother told me to chew a specific herb in her kit that she had, and I can remember everything. Well... nearly everything. I remember my mother and I helping keep lands safe from creatures and writing down the information. When she did it, I was in this room with her. I remember her holding my hands as she told me I looked just like my father. I remember her telling me to always do what Volseggir said and make him think I admired him, so as not to let him become suspicious. She hated him."

"That's it then!" Wolflock clapped. "She would have hidden any information we needed in a book Volseggir would never pick up. If he were ever to find this library, she needed to make sure your plans were safe."

Wolflock raced around the library again, running his fingers along the spines of the books as his eyes flit across their titles. Finally, his eyes stopped on one titled Polinmaedi Mín, Astin Mín. "My Patience, My Love" by B.O. He drew out the book. It was filled with handwritten love poems from a man to a woman.

... Although the dark of the night fills my soul,
I shall always have a campfire for you.
I am not man nor beast, but a walker between.
Take no pity on me, for you are the delights I have
seen...
... Cursed am I that I see not the sun,
But you are the light, you are my one...
... Blood, hunger, voracious rage,
Soothed with a mere memory.
Never in danger. Never to slay...

"These poems are from a vampire to a human woman," Wolflock muttered as he flicked through them. Right at the very back of the book was a different handwriting.

Lucimpus the 15th of Nibit'ling Ickst
I know not if we will succeed, but, if we don't, all
would have been lost, anyway. I have done my best and, as
long as we don't run out of the wild lettuce before Winter, I
will be able to pretend I am his friend. Blandt, if you find
this and I am gone, know that we have a noble cause. You
must finish it. Save the guild, so what happened to your

peaceful father won't happen to anyone else. The guild
must go to the university, or he will take it all.

    If you run out of lettuce, there is more growing at my
cottage. I have a small, dried box of it by my fountain.

    I love you.

    If you visit the fountain, destroy the note.

    Wolflock waited as Blandt and Mothy finished the note over his shoulder. The room grew chilly as a few of the sconces burnt out.

    "This... can't be right. The date..." Blandt gripped his head in pain. "It doesn't make any sense. How can my mother be dead if she was helping me plan to sell the guild to Mystentine in the last few years?"

    "And how can you have a naming certificate dated thirty years ago when you're only seventeen, but have memories of years beyond that?" Wolflock pressed. "What was the last thing you remember about this affair?"

    Blandt scrunched up his face and paced around the room, massaging his thick, brown hair. "I remember... Volseggir's room. I was looking for something in particular; where he was planning on taking over next. I found letters. He was aiming for the entire Restöfundsjúkum hamlet. I found letters from the people who live there telling him to get lost. Then I found-"

"Blandt!" one child from earlier ran down the tunnel and toppled into him. "Volseggir is looking for you."

"Huh? Why?"

"He wants to know where you found the horse outside. He looks like he's seen a ghost."

Wolflock felt a thread snap into place. The carriage was from the Hunters' Guild. Of course Volseggir would remember it. It made Wolflock wonder if the horse was the one who had always drawn the carriage, and if they had sold her with it.

"Come on. I'd better introduce you to him before dinner, anyway."

Blandt led the three of them back to the longhouse, where they waited for the coast to be clear before sneaking out to where the other children were circulating, waiting for food. Wolflock saw they looked worse off than most of the street urchins he had seen in Plugh, Corl or Creast. He could tell they braided their hair to stop it from getting filthy. One of the younger boy's hairs was singed and had developed into a matted rug around his ears. Their clothes were torn and restitched over and over.

"Take a seat. I'll be back soon. We'll talk more after dinner. Don't let Volseggir know we know anything," Blandt whispered over their shoulders as they sat on logs by the firepit.

"Do you take us for fools? We came into this even more prepared than you. We need to get into his room," Wolflock hissed.

"Shh," Blandt hissed back, cuffing Wolflock up the back of the head. "I'll be back."

Mothy grabbed Wolflock's shirt sleeve as he moved to retaliate. "He is so singularly annoying."

"It might be the fact that he acts like an adult even though he's in a teenager's body," Mothy offered, chuckling.

"What's so funny?"

"He's just like you."

Wolflock scoffed and stood up, making his way to where Blandt disappeared. As he approached the door, he heard barrels rolling.

"This is the last of the potatoes?" Blandt asked, out of sight.

"Of course it's not. There's plenty more in the fields," came a raspy, sandpaper voice.

"The frost isn't going to let us get through for much longer, though."

"You'll just have to dig harder then, won't you? All of you slacking off like that," the scratchy voice spat.

"We could set up a deer hunt. Or set some rabbit traps to get meat to dry by-"

"No. No hunting. They're not ready."

"But I've been training them-"

"I said no." the voice growled. "And no more training. No point. The university is buying us up, anyway."

Blandt fell quiet. "I... found something. I found a certificate with my name on it. It said it was from thirty years ago."

Volseggir stopped and the kitchen storage room fell silent. "Where'd you find a thing like that?"

"I... now don't be mad, but I went off the grounds to see if I could snag us a deer and found an old chest by the trails."

"I'll be mad later that you went off the grounds. Those old certificate writing folk were always drunk on celebration mead. Probably confused and stupid. Just like Retta."

Blandt stayed silent, but Wolflock could tell it had upset him.

"Now, listen here, boy. Our way of life and how we hunt is important. We aren't going to be able to pass it on if a bunch of paper pushing cloaked kitten takes over what we do. I know you don't always like my methods, but you're young. You'll realise I'm right. And, if not..." Wolflock heard Volseggir exhale sharply. Wolflock heard nothing for a few seconds, but, when he peeked around the door, he could only see a crotchety old man wiping Blandt's face with a kitchen rag. Blandt hadn't been crying or sweating, though. His face was dry and he looked dizzy.

"That's my boy. Now, you're going to forget everything about this certificate, about everything outside the guild. You're going to be a good apprentice for the rest of the day and tell me everything tomorrow after I initiate the new recruits."

Wolflock watched the old man open a pouch at his hip and sprinkle something over three of the bowls.

"Now, take this to Retta and these two to the two new ones."

Wolflock stepped away from the door and hurried back to Mothy, who had started an in-depth conversation with Retta beside him.

"... And so what you're saying is that you can choose to be in a state of success until you fail, or a state of failure until you succeed? Retta that is so philosophical. Do you use dandelions in your tea? It adds a fantastic flavour and is great for the blood."

"... Blood?" Retta gurgled, blinking up at Mothy with a glimmer of recognition over her tired old face.

Wolflock sat tight up against Mothy on the log. "Volseggir put something in our soup. We can't eat it. He put it in Retta's too. I think she might know something and he's trying to keep her sedated."

"Retta knows a lot of things," Mothy snorted, as if he and Retta had secrets. Wolflock raised an eyebrow, but Mothy just wiggled his head as if he enjoyed knowing something Wolflock didn't.

Blandt wobbled over to them, giving them their bowls with no spoons with a slow, confused movement. As Volseggir walked out of the kitchen storage into the main hall, he stopped to yell at the wrestling children, giving Wolflock the chance he needed to tip his bowl into the firepit. He turned, satisfied with his sleight of hand, then turned to Mothy and Retta, who casually sipped theirs.

"What are you doing? I told you-"

"And I told you. Retta showed me a secret. Don't fret. I'll be fine."

The room fell silent as Volseggir sat down. Everyone in the hall watched as the guild master began eating. Blandt sat next to Volseggir with glazed eyes.

"So you want to join the guild, eh? Got any skills?" Volseggir spat into the fire.

"Uh... not really." Wolflock shrugged.

"Got some pretty clothes on you. Did you steal 'em? Or does your family have land around here?"

"Down South near Creast. There's a big lumbermill there our family owns. We came up here to train because the Nokken have been scaring our workers. We wanted to keep the town safe." Wolflock let the lie roll off his tongue and he watched Volseggir click his tongue against his gums, satisfied with the response.

"It's hard work living and training here. Early starts, late nights. Lots of danger."

"That's what we came for," Wolflock tried to laugh, but it came out forced. To clear the tension, he coughed.

"That's a pretty bangle you have there."

"Oh this? Some old lady coming up the road said to give a message to her sister. We have seen no one, so I guess it's a gift bangle, right?"

Volseggir broke into a long wheezy cackle, slapping his leg. He thought the joke was so funny. While he laughed, Retta cooed, reaching across Mothy to take Wolflock's arm, running her fingers over it as if it were glittering diamonds and gold.

"Why so few students? I heard the Hunters' Guild was huge and prestigious." Mothy asked, swallowing. He chewed something that muffled his voice.

Volseggir growled. "Ah, the people here are fools. They think the training is too hard and that the apprentices don't get enough knowledge from books. Bah. Now I'm only given the broken ones and the orphans." He waved his knotted hand around the room in disgust. "Not even the orphanages want this lot, so it's up to me to extend my charity."

The children around the hall shrank down and avoided making eye contact. Their meek postures made Wolflock seethe. He couldn't stand to see an old monster lord his power over those who relied on him.

"This lot looks like someone could teach them well. I learned a little trick about putting milk and honey out for brownies and peanut butter for goblins, which helped stop them from stealing knick knacks around the house," Wolflock said as he pretended to drink from his bowl.

Volseggir froze, glaring at Wolflock. "We're in the business of killing monsters. Not teaching people how to defend themselves. How are we meant to make a living if every farmer and their dog can ward off what's meant to be our job?"

"Education never ends."

"Education isn't profitable." Volseggir growled. After another suffocating silence, he threw his bowl into the fire, making the room flinch. "Bed. Now."

He got to his feet and scowled around the room. "Blandt, take this pair to bed. You're the only two allowed to eat leftovers tonight."

The old man left and headed outside by the front entrance. The eight children didn't clean up, they just put their bowls on the ground and fought over who would sleep where.

"Which one is his room, Blandt?" Mothy asked.

"Huh?"

"His room. Volseggir's room?"

"I don't follow."

"Don't bother, Mothy. The Guild Master did something to him. He told him to behave and forget everything."

Blandt sat down beside Retta and Wolflock noted a clear similarity between their faces. The same, blank look.

"Shouldn't we help the children get into safe places to sleep? I didn't like how Volseggir spoke to them," Mothy frowned, watching seven of the eight children squabble while Groalani snuck out after Volseggir.

"It's fine. I know which room is his. Find out what you can from the children. I'm going to sift through his room and see what I can put together while he's out. Say 'blubber' loudly if you see him come back."

"Sounds like a plan."

"Oh, and make sure you keep your things on you. If Volseggir gets volatile, we may have to make a run for it."

"After I'm done making sure the rest are safe, I'll get the horse ready. She normally runs at night, so I expect she's eager to go."

Wolflock nodded and smiled to his friend before slipping into the largest, most decorated door with a huge yeti head looming over it. The room was dusty but organised. The immense bed covered in furs took up most of the room, with a shelf embedded in the wall covered with papers. Wolflock smoothed the scrunched-up papers on top, finding letters apologising for addressing him incorrectly and that no one informed them he was their new correspondent. Older letters suggested Maret had been their correspondence up until last year.

Letters with similar postal stamps and handwriting were laid, stacked to the side, unopened. Volseggir refused to acknowledge any mail coming from Mystentine University. Wolflock could tell he ignored the letters to gain more time. Every time he had opened a letter from the University it was them adjusting their price to compensate for the new land he'd gained.

He's trying to rort them for all he can.

He kept the deeds to eight properties and the guildhall in a neat pile. *Jarnsmidur, Jarngmindur, Gullgerda, Koopora, Ritfong, Byfingadil, Fatnadari, Laeknir.* Eight names. *Blacksmith, farrier, alchemist, cooper, stationer, builder, clothier, doctor.* Eight valuable professions.

Beside them lay letters pleading from each of the

families for the Hunters' Guild to help them with dangerous creatures. Some had sent letters again and again, trying to bargain with the price. Volseggir waited until each one said most of the family had been driven away by the monsters. When they were on the verge of complete destruction, Volseggir would swoop in and save the day for the highest price, resulting in the family selling him their land to pay the bill.

Underneath were the adoption papers for each of the children. He couldn't see anything for Blandt. Then, he found a collection of partially filled out adoption papers. No names, but the details of the properties the nameless children came from were completed.

He was planning to take over more land and collect the children, so he owns it. That would keep putting up the price for Mystentine University and delay the purchase of the guild. Surely, arrogance and wanting to keep the guild his wasn't the only driving factor? This was far too organised and elaborate to just be an ego boost.

Wolflock sifted through the notes, catching one that left a grainy feeling on his fingers. He gave it a flick and, in the grey light of his bone match, he saw purple dust scatter across the room. The purple was all too familiar. Lady Mind Master.

Vol

Stop being an idiot. You can't feed it to people. Even I don't trust what it will do. If you want to kill them, up the does. Let me know if it works on your monsters. I know you struggle with anything that requires any kind of mental effort, so read this carefully. This is science. Not magic. You blow it in their face and tell them what you want them to do. Even a simpleton like you can manage that. Destroy this letter after you've memorised it. Trost, I hope you can read.

I'll be passing through before Winter. Don't do anything stupid until I can give you the proper instruction.

Astraxis

Wolflock glared at the page. That name again. The one who slipped away from him in Creast. The 'A' from Parihaan's smuggling agreement. Lady Mind Master powder followed him everywhere.

He clenched the note in his fist and shoved it into his pocket. This evidence was his. He was going to stop Astraxis. He was going to clean up his poison. To make the land that he walked along safe again. Mothy and these children wouldn't be in danger anymore. Wolflock would undo all the hurt that man had strewn across his journey.

He shook with rage at this paper trail of injustice and crime. In an instant, it was washed away by the realisation that hung before him. A tapestry pinned to the wall above Volseggir's bed fluttered, rippling the image of an enormous fortress on a crude map between Mystentine and Creast.

He wants to build a fortress...

Images of an army ravaging the creatures of the land, trampling forests, and laying siege to Mystentine crammed the borders.

... to dominate the land. This man is a lunatic. Delusional. He has no intention of selling the guild to Mystentine. He's going to take their money and fund this ridiculous plan.

"Wanting to train, were you?" growled a raspy voice from the doorway. "Well, here's your first lesson."

Wolflock whipped around and lunged out of the way as Volseggir swung a sword down exactly where he stood. The dark-haired boy rolled across the bed and fell onto the floor on the other side. He had to get to the door, but the savage guild master blocked his way.

"Don't snoop. Don't read."

Wolflock snarled back, his eyes darting around, gauging wherever there could be an opening. "I've never been good at stupid rules."

"Don't. Call. Me. Stupid. Boy!" Volseggir swung again and again, backing Wolflock further into the corner.

His hand hit a fox skin hanging on the wall. On the other side, he felt a decorative shield on the side table. The old man was slim enough to block most of the door, but, with the right distraction, Wolflock would minimise his aim and, with a sturdy object, he could deflect the hit if it struck true. Then the run to the carriage would be easy.

"You're a steady little pest, aren't you? After I've finished with you, I'll make sure your friend doesn't even remember your name."

Wolflock gripped the fox skin, tore it down from the wall and threw it with as much force as he could to blind him. With his left hand, he snatched up the decorative shield and charged for the door. He bashed into Volseggir, sending him into the doorframe. The old man swung his blade. It clashed with the decorative shield, shattering it and jolting Wolflock's hand.

The wild eyes of the old villain bulged as he tore the fox pelt from his face and he plunged his sword forward, catching Wolflock's right arm as it glanced off the doorframe. Wolflock slipped passed and although his arm seared with white hot pain, he raced forward, gritting his teeth. His feet pounded against the stone as Volseggir collected himself and chased after him.

Wolflock flung the entrance door open and slammed it back, hoping it would stay shut, but the old hunter continued the chase.

"Go! Go! Go!" Wolflock shouted, seeing Mothy holding the door open from the carriage.

"Lockie, come on!"

The black mare started to move, climbing to a gallop in moments. Wolflock aimed his run ahead of the horse and leaped. He fell short of the carriage and heard the sword swish at his back, but Mothy's hand gripped his arm and hoisted him into the carriage. The moment Wolflock was in, the blond boy thumped on the carriage wall.

"Khra! Get us out of here! To Mystentine!" He turned back to Wolflock. "You got what you need? I sure hope so, because I am done with this case."

"We've got one more place, Mothy. Khra! To Restöfundsjúkum. We need to know what happened the night Runar went missing."

CHAPTER 9

Resting Bones

The carriage rattled them around as it flew down the road. Mothy stared, deadpan, at Wolflock, rocking from side to side with the motion of the compartment.

"Lockie..."

Wolflock threw up his hands and winced at the pain in his right arm. "Look, Mothy, I know. I understand. This is all my fault. I'm the one who chose Khra's carriage. The old woman was upset by me. I pushed to investigate this whole thing and I'm the one sitting here with an injured arm. I am sorry about you hitting your head at the inn, though."

Mothy opened his mouth, but Wolflock talked over him. "I can't leave, though. And, even if we went to Mystentine, I'd just be transported magically back to Creast. Those children have been cheated out of their land and it has decimated their families. A place that should be giving the locals information to keep them safe is destroying them for profit and I will not stand by while these people, and this entire region, remain powerless to bring justice to the fiend ruling the Hunters Guild."

Mothy's expression didn't change, but his eyes moved from steely grey to bright blue.

"Can I speak?"

Wolflock gestured apologetically.

"I was going to say-"

"I also found evidence that Volseggir has been using the purple powder from Astraxis and they've been corresponding for months." Wolflock cut across quickly before pressing his fist to his lips to show he had finished.

Mothy eyed him, unable to keep a smile from creeping into the corners of his mouth. "As I was going to say, I spoke with the children. They are sickly, underfed, filthy, and they all have lice. Blandt has been going out to find medicinal herbs for them to make the Winter survivable for them. There was no way we were going to leave them without help. I thought we could get to Mystentine and alert the authorities to come and help this region. I'd get us lodging and some work for when you came back from Creast. While you were there, you could ask the authorities there to help and they would stop Volseggir from both sides."

"That's... that's not a bad plan." Wolflock put his hand on Himi's sapphire in his pocket. He didn't want to part with it. Not for something this foolish. And not to such a mean old lady. "We still have two days left before the half moon."

"Did you have a plan? Also, did Volseggir stab your arm? You're not bleeding. What happened?"

"He swiped me while I escaped his room. I found the deeds of all the land he's stolen, the letters from the families begging for help with monsters, and pre-filled adoption papers for the children in the land he intends to gain control over. I also found a note from Astraxis telling him how to use the purple power. It was covered in traces of it. Old Finnes'Anna learns everything I've learned when this bangle goes back to her. I thought if we solved the case, she would get the information she's after without us losing distance or Himi's stone."

"That is a better plan. Let's call mine the emergency plan. Let me see your arm."

"Last resort plan. If we solve the case, the old

woman won't be able to trick anyone else out of their belongings." Wolflock held out his arm for Mothy, who checked the cut.

"You're not bleeding. What did he hit you with?"

"His sword. How am I not bleeding?"

"It looks like you've been burnt. Are you sure it wasn't a hot poker?"

"I know a sword when I see one. Never mind. It means the wound is clean. When we get to the hamlet, we have to find Maret's old house and see if anyone knew where the trap for the bubak had been set. That's where Runar's last note was made. That may be where he left the pages of the back of his book, and that's where we'll find out what happened to him."

"And Maret?"

Wolflock frowned, bundling a blanket on his lap. "There was the naming certificate in the inn, the book of poems in the guild, and Blandt's fragmented memories. Beyond that, her old house is the best place we can look."

"How long until we get there?" Mothy tried to mask a yawn.

Wolflock felt his body grow heavy as the adrenaline finally plummeted. "If I remember correctly from the map, which I do, we'll be there a few hours from morning. We should be able to find a spot for Khra's horse away from the hamlet. We don't want to spook the people there."

"And the horse is definitely spooky," Mothy chuckled, curling up against his bag.

"Beautiful, though. The frightening things often are."

Wolflock heard Mothy make a response, but drifted into sleep before it registered. Instead of sleep, he had terrible visions of shadows bearing fangs dripping with blood. A flaming blade cut through the shadows until his back pressed into a corner. Wolflock's heart raced, and, in the darkness, he saw a spindly pumpkin faced monster pouncing after the flaming sword. He knew, any second now, it would look at him and there was nothing he could do. The suspense choked him.

The sword dug into the shadowed wall beside his head and the heat was barely an inch from burning him. Then the hollow eyes of the pumpkin turned to him. He knew what was about to happen.

It rushed forward, and Wolflock gasped, throwing the blanket off and blinking in the warm sunlight. Mothy stared at him with tired grey eyes from across the compartment, still curled up against his bag.

"Nightmares for you, too?"

Wolflock gathered his bearings and caught his

breath. He nodded, falling back into the corner of the seat. "That scarecrow thing. Shadows. Flaming sword. It followed it. Is this case doing something to us?"

"I thought the carriage was haunted. I dreamed about being back at the mill."

Wolflock felt the warm air in the carriage turn to ice. He knew what that meant to Mothy.

"You're safe, you know? You're over a thousand miles from all that."

"And you're not being chased by shadows. Doesn't make the dreams any less frightening." Mothy dropped the blanket on his seat and stepped out of the carriage.

Wolflock watched him leave. They'd both had a hard day and night. It was best to give him space. He looked out of the window and saw a log cabin with heather growing over the thatching.

Khra took us all the way to the cottage?

Wolflock stepped out and saw that the horse and Khra were nowhere to be seen. Mothy had flopped on his back in the overgrown wildflowers filling the fenced in front yard.

"I feel better now," he called from the blanket of dandelions. "Sorry for being grumpy."

Wolflock chuckled. The scene before him was so strange. They had seen so much darkness and obscurity over the past few days that the beautiful garden in the late Autumn sun felt like a balm for the soul. The only thing that felt out of place were the posters rustling in the breeze. Someone had plastered them over the fence, windows, walls and carriage shed.

"Do all witches have cottages like this?" Mothy's disembodied voice rose out of the flowers.

"All the ones I know. Except for Finnes'Anna, of course."

"If being a doctor doesn't work out, I'm becoming a witch, then. We need to meet more witches. She's got burdock, rosehip, that pink daisy thing that's good for colds, liquorice and nettles everywhere."

Wolflock sat on the front step, folding his hands with his elbows on his knees. "I'm sure there are plenty at Mystentine. Everywhere has witches, though."

He picked up one of the faded posters caught in the shrub growing over the path next to him. A grim image of a red-eyed shadowy fanged creature met his gaze with the words:

MISSING GOATS?

YOUR BEST DEFENCE AGAINST VAMPIRES IS THE HUNTERS' GUILD. CAN'T AFFORD US? USE STRINGS OF GARLIC UNTIL YOU CAN.

Wolflock frowned at the poster, wondering if Volseggir had the children make these to get more work from the locals. He scrunched it up and lobbed it into the patch Mothy had laid in.

"I saw these on the trees last night. They cover most of the road between here and the guild. I didn't know what they said, but they looked just like this."

"He's not particularly good at business. When people are so belligerent, they fall hard. I'm going to look inside."

Wolflock rose and tried the front door. It was locked. From the feel of the door handle, the door was latched with a sturdy bolt. Not something he could force open or slide a pen knife through. Maret had been very security conscious.

He tried the windows, but they were latched too. He even tried breaking one in order to unlatch it, but the stone he picked up bounced off with a wave of magic.

She'd warded the place against unwanted entry. Clever.

The shed door rattled with a breeze, and he made his way there. The old carriage shed had an awning and empty troughs for horses to be stabled. Khra and the horse weren't there, though. Wolflock opened the side door and saw it hadn't been necessary. The North facing double doors were shattered, which had allowed Khra and his horse to find a sunless place to rest during the day. The rest of the shelter had been completely enclosed, boarded up so not a glitter of sunlight came through.

The giant black mare and her driver laid in the middle of the shed on the old dirt floor.

"You knew about this place, didn't you, Khra?" Wolflock asked as he ran his hands over the carriage repair tools. They had been disused for decades, but he thought the brittle wooden handles looked familiar. Several paintings hung around the shelter, all of a beautiful black horse. At first, they were in the sun while the horse was a foal. A prominent one was a man with a similar dark brown shade of hair to Blandt resting his forehead on the horse's. After that, none were painted, but old sketches of the horse lay scattered in the corner.

Khra made a rattling noise in his throat under his hat. "Yes."

"Any reason for this place?"

The horse nuzzled under Khra's hat. "This place... is safe... for me."

No sunlight. Away from prying eyes. Main doors facing away from the road. Abandoned.

"Did you know Maret?"

Khra stayed silent before he let out a long sigh. "This is home."

Wolflock didn't understand if that meant yes or no, but he had no chance to ask. He heard voices outside and Mothy's apologetic tone.

"I'm sorry. I didn't think anyone lived here anymore. We came to see-"

"You need to leave now. It isn't safe for a child like yourself and your big fancy carriage to be near this place. It's haunted, you know?"

Wolflock poked his head out to see a middle-aged woman with a child on her hip approaching Mothy. He thought he'd better step out before his friend said something to give away anything they needed to keep secret.

"Sorry, ma'am. We were told by Maret's sister that she might be here. We're in need of assistance, you see. I thought she just might be out collecting mushrooms or herbs."

"Maret doesn't live here anymore. She moved thirty years ago. What did you need her for?" The suspicious tone the woman spoke to Wolflock in had a trace of inquisitiveness. He saw she had a bag on her hip and her fingers were green from picking fresh herbs. The medallions holding her dress straps had sigils on them, and she wore a string of rune stones on her belt.

A witch's apprentice. Interesting.

"Her sister said it was best to meet her here. The Hunters' Guild isn't anyone's favourite in these parts. I know a few friends of ours have come for help during the evenings when times are hard. Finnes'Anna never mentioned an apprentice. I'm Wolflock."

He reached out his hand and waited for her to shake it. He could tell she didn't know whether or not to be astounded, or even more suspicious.

"Why did you leave the posters up?"

Mothy rocked back and leaped to his feet, bowing to the woman. "I'm Mothy. Don't mind my friend. He's all business all the time. What was your name?"

The woman's face relaxed into a smile. "I'm Lagatha and this is Mirret. Come in. We'll have some tea. I'll see if I can help you boys with what you need."

Lagatha drew out a long necklace that chinked with keys and unlocked the cottage door with a thunk. She put her hand on the round handle and hummed a little song. The wood of the door glowed green along the cracks and lines in the wood, then faded with a little pop. The child rushed over to a chest in the corner and began playing with the toys she drew out of it, while Lagatha lit the fire in the stove and put the kettle on.

The boys followed her in. Mothy helped her with the fire and kettle while Wolflock looked around. Strings of shrivelled onions and sticks of herbs that had long turned to dust hung from the rafters. A thick layer of dust covered everything except three things. The fireplace, the kitchen bench, and an old bookcase filled with handwritten notes stuffed into grimoires.

He watched as Lagatha carefully moved containers back to their original circles left in the dust. She gripped the lids and corks from the sides, leaving the dust on top. Wolflock wondered if her behaviour was a compulsion or if she was trying to keep the house looking as deserted as possible.

"There we go. Chamomile and ginger are a good breakfast tea. Helps stimulate the appetite." Wolflock waited for her to take a sip before taking his own. "I left the posters up because I had nothing to help the people that came here anymore. Maret used to let weary night travellers come and drink from her fountain, but the stone in it went missing and it dried up. She left a note, but then I heard the people that came through have gone missing. I wanted to deter them."

"How long has that been going on for?" Wolflock asked.

"She hasn't been back at her cottage for a year now.

That's how long the disappearances have been happening for, as well. I've scried for her, but I'm getting mixed messages."

Wolflock took his tea over to the stone sink in the shape of two giant shells above one another. It looked like it belonged outdoors, but it had been plumbed with a hand pump and the pipes lead to a drain outside. Along the base of the sink was a brownish red stain, except for where a flat, fist sized, octagonal gemstone had once been. That stone remained clear.

"What do you mean by mixed messages?" Mothy inquired, as he sipped his tea, smacking his lips. "This is delicious."

"Thank you. I use runes for my scrying. I am getting ambiguous answers. Sometimes, they say she is dead, but not fully, other times they say she isn't. I looked for her location and I get the Hunters Guild, the cottage and a strange travelling piece or two."

"Are you sure you're reading them correctly? Divination can be a fickle practice," Wolflock warned as he found a shredded note in the top shell. Blandt destroyed the note, then. Just like Maret asked him to. How did he not remember any of this?

"I'm very confident in my runes. I've been successful with all of my readings for the townspeople.

And for Maret, before this last year," Lagatha sniffed, lifting her chin. "That's not all, though. The villagers are convinced vampires have been killing their goats since Maret left. Normally, the runes can tell me what it is. Vampires don't leave goats full of blood in the field. Whenever we have had wayward ones, or frightened ones, they just take one and drain it. Whatever is killing them now is leaving them massacred."

"What do you think it is?" Wolflock asked as he brought the shredded note to the table, piecing it back together.

"Well, at first I thought it was a bubak. That's what did this last time. But the runes say it's nothing that is beast or aberration."

"So it's a human." Wolflock offered bluntly.

Mothy coughed, eyeing him off and warning him to mind his manners. Lagatha sighed and rolled her cup between her garden-stained hands.

"I can't say that to the villagers. They're so frightened. If they think it's one of them, they will never recover. Restöfundsjúkum will tear itself apart. They're hanging on by a thread as it is."

"And they'll never trust outsiders again if they find out it's one of the Hunters Guild," Wolflock muttered.

They sat in tense silence for a few moments,

wondering how they could save the situation, when Lagatha jumped up.

"I'm so sorry. You came all this way to see Maret and get her help, and all we've spoken about is the village's problems. Let me make more tea and tell me what troubles you. I'll see if I can help."

Wolflock looked to Mothy as his friend collected the mismatched teacups.

"Well... we needed to learn about this bubak creature. We're looking for Finnes'Anna's husband. He was last seen here forty years ago, and we found he had laid a trap for one of these things."

Lagatha sighed. "I'm terribly sorry. You're not the first people who have come through. How many days do you have left?"

Wolflock rolled the pewter bangle along the table. "We have until the moon rises tomorrow night. I'm not sure when the spell will end that evening, but we have at least until the half moon. If Maret only went missing last year, why did she never tell her sister about Runar or herself?"

Lagatha sighed. "I said she went missing last year, but, in truth, after she had her son, she didn't want to risk any harm coming to the rest of her family. She kept everything very secret. I was only a child when the last bubak attacked and Maret's entire focus has been on keeping the region safe ever since. At first, she also wanted to find out what happened to Runar. That's why she got close to the Hunters Guild. Then she got married and had her son. I think she realised the guild was rotting from the inside, so she took me on as an apprentice in order to keep the hamlet safe. She's been losing her faculties ever since she lost her husband in the fire at the inn."

"So Blandt's father died in the fire?" Wolflock asked. He didn't remember seeing any bodies or bones at the burnt down inn.

Lagatha nodded sadly. "I think that's one reason she let the other night travellers come to her house. She wanted to keep them safe and do what she couldn't do for her husband. Her visits became less and less frequent, though, and she seemed to lose huge parts of her memory. The last time I saw her, she warned me that the guild master was up to something, but I feel I've been powerless to stop it."

Wolflock's nose wrinkled in disgust. "He seems to be doing that to the entire region. Why hasn't the Guard stepped in?"

"They know nothing about it. The guild master put up wards that alert him to travellers on the roads in and out of the areas he controls, and he vets any of the letters that go through the post. The only postal station is at the Hunter's Guild. He changes the letters and no one outside the area thinks the situation is that bad. The people are helpless to protect themselves. I know the people in the hamlet would sell their land, but he only pays a pittance, and just before Winter, it isn't enough to get them through. Most of them have been here for generations, and some are too old to travel that far."

Wolflock finished putting the shredded note together. It read:

Don't fret, the gemstone is safe. Come to the hunters' guild and into the tomb, and you'll be able to drink in safety.
Maret'Anna Oviru

"Tell me what you know about bubaks and the last time they attacked the hamlet. If we find out what happened to Runar and Maret, we may be able to help the people of the region. With the right evidence, our horse and carriage can get past the Guard Posts Volseggir controls and we can go straight to Mystentine." Wolflock fiddled with the bangle. And, maybe, Creast.

"Like I said, I was only a child. I remember

everyone being terrified. Bubaks are shadows that inhabit human shaped effigies. Dolls, wooden toys, mannequins, even scarecrows. The stronger they get, the larger the container they need. Once they're in it, they can cast illusions to make you think the thing they're in is changing. Like a mannequin growing knife hands or a toy doll growing extra legs. A little boy's puppet was said to turn its strings into needles before it tried to strangle him and ran off into the forest when it was stopped. Then our sheep and goats started going missing."

"Why is it always goats around here?" Mothy shook his head.

"I don't think there is enough grass for cattle or larger herd animals to be kept in the same place for long. Your runes said the current thing killing your livestock wasn't a bubak, though, wasn't it?" Wolflock clarified.

"That's right. It is creating a lot of fear, though. Maret wrote in her books here that the bubak feeds off fear. It's drawn to it and becomes stronger for it. One by one, it will wipe out an entire village to feed."

"How are they created?" Wolflock asked, moving to the bookcase and searching through the grimoires for entries from around that time. He also kept an eye out for things about Runar or the Hunters Guild.

"Maret said they came from a magical child

suffering from too much fear. This one had been feeding on the hamlet for weeks. She called in her favourite two hunters to help her end it. Normally she tried to capture and understand the creatures, but this one... She said bubaks were irredeemable. I think this event made her think this way. They set the trap in the back paddock, and she told the town to continue to celebrate her wedding. I was at the bonfire dancing that night and Maret never spoke about what happened. All I know is that she didn't come back that evening."

"Let's see the area where they laid the trap, then."

Lagatha led the boys out into the back paddock and within sixty feet of the forest that marked the edge of the property. In the middle of the space stood an empty tall post shaped like a 'T' where they hung the scarecrow.

"They did this same thing at the inn, didn't they?" Wolflock asked, pinching his chin between his thumb and index finger.

"I do remember that one. I had just become Maret's apprentice and the night of her son's naming ceremony we had to clear one out from there."

"And how do you 'clear one out'?" Wolflock looked into the surrounding trees. He saw no movement, but he felt like something watched them.

"You set a trap by putting an empty vessel down

that is a better quality than the one it currently has. They tend to be quite arrogant and think they can control an object much larger. That makes them easy to catch. They have to get used to it and stumble around looking silly. Then you destroy the vessel."

"And you do that how, exactly?"

"The only way to destroy one is for a vampire to bite it and drain its darkness from the vessel. The vampire becomes dangerously hungry as they do it, though, and it can weaken them. Maret only did that here, though. The time at the inn, I'm not sure what happened."

Wolflock ran his mind through his web again. Runar's last entry had been here. That was the only entry that didn't have the phrase Leyndarmal Ad Aftan at the end. The only entry that hadn't been completed. Kept for forty years under Khra's seat, in the carriage branded with the Hunter's Guild insignia. Did he tear the pages out before the attempt to trap the bubak? Or had someone taken them out after? Someone who had taken his possessions off him and found he'd written things in the back of his book that they needed to hide. But what were they?

"Lagatha, you said your scrying is normally accurate, yes?"

"Best in the village," she shrugged with a smile.

Her daughter Mirret clung to her leg, snatching her chubby little hand out at dandelion seeds floating through the air.

"Where are the back pages of this book?" He held the notebook out, his thumb pinning down the pages before the place they were torn out.

Lagatha drew out a large, patterned bib and laid it on the grass. She knelt on one edge to keep it flat in the breeze and placed a chunk of clear quartz on each corner and the book in the middle. She untied the string of rune stones around her waist and slid her hand down it, unthreading them into her palm.

"Is that your question?"

"Yes. Where are these missing pages?" Wolflock said with a firm nod.

She spoke in old Shirth, chanting a spell before throwing down the pieces and gazing over them carefully. "Huh... six miles Northwest. I think it's saying it's at the end of the old hunting track."

"Lead the way," Wolflock grinned, feeling like they had a solid thread to follow.

Lagatha started rethreading her runes. "I can't leave Mirret and she's too young to come with us. Follow the main road and you'll see a river on one side and a track leading North. Follow the track and you'll head true."

Wolflock frowned, but he didn't protest. She'd been so forthcoming with information already.

"I'll get snacks ready," Mothy said thoughtfully.

"Thank you, Lagatha. You've been immeasurably helpful. Merry Part."

She bundled up her things and scooped Mirret onto her hip. "I'll tell the villagers that this is a fool trying to scare us and that they need to keep their flocks close and voices loud. Hopefully that will scare away the guild master, or at least get a few sightings so the villagers can rule out anything unnatural. Merry part, and merry meet again."

Wolflock brushed Khra's horse while Mothy put together a few sandwiches for lunch and the hike ahead. The pair of them set off just after midday. As they walked through the little hamlet of ten houses, they saw strings of garlic hung over everything. Clusters of garlic bulbs hung over fences, gates, doorways, and under window sills. The few people who were out and about fell silent and watched them walk through.

"Should we let them know why we're here? Or see if they know anything else?" Mothy asked.

Wolflock frowned, then turned around and continued to walk backwards. "Lagatha will be along shortly, we're off to find the rogue attacking your livestock. Be merry, good people. Be merry and laugh."

The townsfolk looked astounded, even the chickens in their front yards stopped pecking. Mothy nodded in approval, and they kept walking.

"They're quite worried about the vampires, aren't they?" Mothy commented as they made it through the town and reached the fork by the river and path.

They both stopped, but Wolflock clenched his jaw and stepped off first.

The path was wide enough for a small cart and wound through the forest, curving around old trees, shapely boulders and berry bushes. The path showed a distinct appreciation and respect for the natural riches that neighboured them. Initially, the echo of the babbling stream kept them comforted. It was as if they were on a simple nature walk.

Then the water sound stopped, the birds disappeared, and the sound of the leaves rustling followed them up the trail. The canopy of pine, cypress and snow closed over them and the shadows flickered either side of them. It had a similar feeling to the path to Khra's forest. Wolflock pressed forward. His blue eyes shone with determination, and he didn't slacken the pace, even when his chest buzzed from the fear he tried to squash down.

He ignored Mothy's gasps and exclamations, focusing on the burning cold around his wrist. Finally, they made it to the end of the path and saw a campsite in front of a rocky cave.

"Is this it? I was expecting a treasure chest or a fancy fairy desk." The blond boy commented, tapping the dried, dead petals off a nearby bush.

Wolflock approached the campfire surrounded by stones. The chunks of coal were under layers of leaves and silt. It hadn't been used in years. And, yet, there were signs of life around them. A small makeshift forge and whetstone had been used within the last few weeks. Who would come all this way and not eat, but prepare weapons?

As he trod carefully into the cave, he saw crates stacked to the side. He didn't have a crowbar, so he couldn't open them, but, from the smell, there were medicines, preserved foods and fabrics inside them. All fresh enough to produce a faint smell. Even the ink from the address stamp looked clear and bright.

They're all addressed to the Hunters Guild... Are these the emergency stores Maret had organised? No. These are fresher than a year. Did Blandt organise them and then become mind controlled? He pondered the idea for a few moments, thinking that he'd have to put that thread in place when he saw Blandt next.

Looking around, Wolflock first thought the cave may have been a tunnel as he could see a light at the other end, but, as he approached it, he realised it was a shrine. An undisturbed grave laid before him with a stone plaque set above in a candle filled enclave with a small wooden box at its centre.

Here lies Runar Slatra

Secret Keeper of the Hunter's Guild, loving husband of Finnes'Anna, beloved friend and brother-in-law of Maret'Anna Oviru, best friend of Blyrkjun Oviru.

May your hunt bring you all you need.

Under Maret and Blyrkjun's names, someone had carved one of the Hunter's Guild symbols. Wolflock pulled out his journal and flicked through to where Blandt had written them down.

"Avenge... Maret and Blyrkjun swore to avenge Runar." Wolflock mumbled, turning to Mothy.

"Didn't they slay the bubak, though?"

"They did... three highly experienced hunters who laid a trap and yet Runar died..." Wolflock opened the little wooden box from the enclave and grinned as he found the missing pages. It only took him a moment to match them to their torn edges.

"Umm... are those candles magical? Does that mean someone has been here recently?" Mothy swallowed and took out the last pages left in the box that weren't part of the diary.

Wolflock narrowed his eyes at the candles. "They don't look magical. Someone has been here very recently."

He read the pages in the golden candlelight as Mothy took a few steps back and looked anxiously to the entrance.

Relimpus the 14th of Xissyli Sor, 5th year of Queen Circia

I searched in the secret library and found out the witch was right! These weird techniques have soothed some of the creatures we have been slaying. I'll start sharing it with the apprentices. It might keep them out of harm's way. Gods know they need it.

Ferimpus the 20th of Xissyli Sor, 6th year of Queen Circia

Volseggir doesn't like me listening to these witches and keeping notes on what they say, but, as Secret

Keeper, it's my job to make notes of all this. If he had half an ounce of respect for anything, he'd understand that. My role is an ancient one and, just because we don't remember why it exists, it doesn't mean I'm not going to do my best. He owes us a drink for saving his hide.

Quintampus the 10th of Ha'ling Felst, 7th year of Queen Circia

Demons are also in the library catalogue. I only knew a little bit about them, but I've been down here every night, adding to our records and researching what they really are. The possibility for relapse is always strong without constant vigilance from the community. It breaks some families and the afflicted often end up in Ulusai'il or the labyrinth in Ungulerth. No way to tell how old they are either as the human inside stops ageing when the demon consumes them. The ones in Shiriling have been lurking here for hundreds of years. Sometimes it's a mercy to send them back to the great mother, Pelaia.

Relimpus the 28th of Ha'ling Felst, 7th year of Queen Circia

The library has stories of some people befriending trolls and having them protect their land or keeping vagabonds away. They're fairly stupid and it's easy to

convince them of anything if they aren't mad. I might try this out in the Western forests, away from the guild. Witches are also in these books. I wonder if it's something the parents pass down to their children.

Sollempus the 26th of Alung unt te Gaia, 7th year of Queen Circia

I'm hoping that, with these new techniques I'm learning from the library, I'll be able to keep the people safer and I won't have to travel as much anymore. Blyrkjun isn't the new leader, but I'm going to show him the library first and see if it's a good idea to show Volseggir. I'm worried the hot head will burn the books for telling him how wrong he's been all these years.

Sollempus the 18th of Frum'ling St'sol, 9th year of Queen Circia

Blyrkjun was torn to shreds by a clan of feral vampires. They attacked him when he tried to convince them to make a deal. He kept saying that it wasn't their fault, and that they were just hungry. He tried to bite Maret, but she told him off like a dangerous dog. She fed him her blood. He's a vampire. I don't know what to do. I have to tell Volseggir.

Sollempus the 18th of St'lung Luna, 9th year of Queen Circia

I couldn't tell Volseggir about Blyrkjun. It's his personal business and I want to make sure he's fine or not before I set the bear on him. He's my oldest friend. He needs time, and time is what I want to give him. I also spoke to Volseggir about the letters I found. I think he might be trying to steal land by not defending the people on it until they sell it to him for cheap. It's hard to imagine him being that horrible, so I'll give him another chance, too. Finnes'Anna keeps me in a very forgiving mood. She'd be proud of the decisions I made today. I'll tell her when the time is right.

"Mothy, I think we nearly have all the proof we need. Runar was going to confront Volseggir about his dealings just before they set the trap for the bubak. That gives him motive. Runar lived mostly in Creast, so he would have taken the issue to a larger authority that was not in Volseggir's pocket." Wolflock grinned, closing the diary and sliding it into his satchel.

"Lockie... Look at these. How recent are these?"

Mothy's face was deathly pale.

Wolflock took the papers off him and read. The dates were missing, but Wolflock could make out a general timeline. It appeared that the papers had been shoved into the box at random.

In honour of Runar, I refuse to let that vermin destroy these people. Hated or unwanted, I will protect them. I will protect my child...

Stalked the bubak. It grows daily. The people are scared of him and his mess of a guild...

I drove the vampires away. He won't be able to hurt them anymore. I hope they found refuge in Plugh...

The spectre horse is back. Here to torment me for not being able to save her...

I can't tell if I'm afraid or just grieving. The bubak is at ten feet tall now. It doesn't know I'm stalking it. I think...

It's found the guild. The monster keeping those children so frightened drew it right to them. My sword is sharp, and I am full. I have no idea how powerful it will be. Tonight will end it, one way or another.

Wolflock's eyes grew wider as he read.

"How old is that last line?"

Wolflock lifted his thumb from the page. "It's still wet."

CHAPTER 10

Evil Unveiled

They both took off running back down the path and gained speed as they went downhill.

"We didn't see anyone on the path. How could they have passed us?" Mothy shouted.

"He's been living in these woods for years. He probably has his own trails to stay away from people."

Their shoes hit the hard road, and they tore through the middle of town, back to Maret's cottage.

"The sun is setting," Mothy panted as he caught up to Wolflock.

"Excellent! Khra will be ready to go."

As they came up to the carriage, they saw the driver and horse in place, waiting for them.

"We need to go back to the Hunters' Guild. As fast as you can, Khra." Wolflock flung the door open and banged on the roof rapidly to get him going.

Khra's horse whinnied, rearing back and shaking the carriage before yanking it forward with a lightning start. The thunderous hooves flew them forward down the road at nightmarish speeds. The compartment rattled, and the boys held onto their seats as darkness crept over the sky. Wolflock bounced his legs, wanting to run, but they were confined to the tiny compartment.

"What are we going to do when we get there?" Mothy asked after his stomach had settled from the tumultuous ride.

"I'm not sure. I know we need to give the children courage."

"Your bangle, Lockie. Look."

Wolflock had been trying to ignore it. The pewter had produced ice around itself, making his wrist ache, but, more than that, it had pulled on his arm as if it were magnetised to Creast.

He tried the pin again. It lodged into its socket, but turning it did nothing. "We need to save those children. That's all I can focus on at the moment."

"Let's do that then. What's your plan?"

"They all think Volseggir is a bogeyman they can't escape. We can weaken the bubak by getting it to use a new vessel and, while it's getting used to that body, we'll be able to tell the children what we've found, offer them the protection they've needed and reveal Volseggir to be the coward he is."

"Words. Got it. Where are we going to find another scarecrow for the bubak, though?"

Wolflock scrunched up his face as he thought.

"Umm... Gah... Myna would have been good at this. She used to make people-looking things all the time to sneak away. That's it!" Wolflock took off his jacket and started shoving a blanket into it. "Grab those pillows for a chest and a head. We don't have trousers, so we'll make a skirt. Hopefully, we can make it look appealing enough that the monster will just jump into it."

Mothy's eyes lit up, and he took over the design elements of their project until they had a functional dummy.

Khra pulled the carriage into the Hunters' Guild Lane, and the boys prepared themselves. The lights in the guild hall were dim and one of the few lights came from a flash of strange rippling lightning from the Northern side of the property.

"Blandt!" Wolflock shouted as he burst from the door, holding his wine glass lantern high.

"Mothy, we're going to need as much light as we can get. Put the dummy in the field there and get lighting all those sconces. I'll get Blandt to help us."

Mothy jumped to action as Wolflock sped off into the hall.

"Blandt! Blandt, you son of a witch! Get out here."

No one answered. The silence sent a chill through Wolflock.

"They're not here."

He spun around to see a six-and-a-half-foot tall man with brown hair streaked in grey step out of Volseggir's room. He wore a sword as long as Wolflock was tall, and his black cloak moved around him with an untouchable wind. His voice was that of oiled silk, but his deep red eyes and pale skin made Wolflock want to run.

They weren't here. Where else would they have gone? Wolflock thought, dragging his mind back to the maps in Finnes'Anna's tin box. The tomb!

Wolflock raised a finger and waved it at the tall stranger. "You are terrifying. Stay with Mothy and don't be creepy. I'll get the children. Don't give it any more fear to feed off."

Still waving his finger, he set off at a run, then

jogged back. "Where is the tomb?"

The stranger smiled, keeping his lips shut. He raised a long, taloned finger and pointed towards the back of the property.

"Thanks." And he set off again.

Wolflock ran through the graveyard, leaping over graves with old, crumbling headstones. He saw Groalani holding a lit torch as Blandt and Volseggir yelled at each other.

"We're meant to just go down there and hide? That thing will never leave!" Blandt roared.

"Get down there now! I'll deal with it," spat Volseggir as he brandished his heated sword.

"I'm not sealing them in there. It's a death sentence."

"They're going in, with or without you."

"They're my family. They're coming with me. Go back to the hall. I have a place you're all going to be safe-"

Volseggir's face contorted with rage, and he raised his sword, bringing it down towards Blandt's back.

"COWARD!" Wolflock bellowed. Without thinking, he threw out his right arm to block the attack. At first, he thought the icy feeling was shock, but then he realised he was struggling to hold back the weight of the blade as it battled with the ice growing out of the pewter bangle.

"Wolflock!" Blandt gasped.

The children stared at him with wide eyes as he held his shaking arm firm. Volseggir's eyes blazed with shock and loathing.

"You!"

"I won't let you kill any more innocent people. All the misfortune that has fallen on this guild is your fault, and I will not stand by and let your wreak havoc any longer!"

Wolflock thrust his arm forward, snapping the ice and crunching it into Volseggir's nose. The old man reeled back, giving Wolflock the moment he needed to grab the ball of ice that had formed around the blade, tossing it beyond some gravestones. It caught onto a leather cord from around Volseggir's neck and something else went flying with a metallic clink on the stone graves.

"You," the guild master sneered, "come onto my land and assault me, raving this nonsense, and expect these pitiful brats to follow you away? They do what I tell them to do."

"No. Not anymore." Wolflock turned to the children. "He is responsible for the deaths of your families. He refused to help them when they needed it most until it was only each of you left, then swooped in and took your land. There are pre signed adoption papers ready to do the same to other children. Blandt, he's been controlling your mind with a toxic purple powder. He made you forget who you were and what your mission was. To restore the Hunters' Guild. This fiend killed your uncle. He burned down the inn on the day of your naming ceremony to try and kill your parents. He's been luring bubaks to villages to extort them."

"You have no proof!" The gritty old man bared his teeth, gripping the tombstone in front of him for support.

"I have all the proof the authorities need. I have Runar's journal, your letter from Astraxis, the testimonies of all these children, your flaming sword, the pouch of powder on your hip, and the witnesses of most of your crimes. If that wasn't enough, when this bracelet takes me back to Creast, I'll bring the entire guard marching through here. They'll just have to look at the state of the children and you'll be taken away for good."

Volseggir's beady eyes darted to his sword and back to Wolflock as fast as fire, but Wolflock just stepped up to the old man. He had to show the children that their monster was just a frail old coward.

"There's just one thing I wanted to know. I wasn't

going to desecrate Runar's grave to find out," he said in a low tone, but loud enough for everyone to hear over the thunder cracking at the edge of the property. "Did you actually look him in the eye as he died, or did you stab him in the back like the piece of dirt you are?"

Volseggir's features writhed with the last flames of a defeated man, but his hand flashed to his pocket. Wolflock jumped back too late to dodge the knife coming for his gut, but a purple fire wreathed itself around his wrist and held it taught. Wolflock followed the string of magical fire and saw the glowing violet eyes of Retta.

"Put him in the tomb. We're going to hunt a monster," said Blandt, standing tall.

Groalani tied Volseggir's hands behind his back with a horse lead and the children pushed him into the old tomb, locking the iron gate with wide smiles. The blacksmith, Tultra, picked up Volseggir's sword and carried it with confidence.

But they didn't last for long as the thunder sent a streak of lightning overhead and the protective ward shattered. Retta cried out and collapsed. Blandt caught her just in time.

"Make sure she's in a safe place." Wolflock told him as they passed through the training field. "Now, you may see something that looks very scary. It is not real. I can't stress that enough. It is an illusion meant to make you afraid. Courage may weaken it. We may need you to bite it."

Blandt nodded and shouted to the others, "You are all part of the hunters' guild, and this is just a monster to hunt. Focus on all the times you felt brave. Focus on all the times you felt strong. You have to show it you're not afraid. That makes it weaker."

The children looked hesitant, but they nodded, looking at each other for support.

"Groalani, take Retta. Boys, remember that big secret room you found us in through the storage room? If things go poorly, take everyone there. Sing songs and read books and have fun. We're going to take care of this, now."

The two boys they'd seen earlier looked determined. Although Wolflock could sense most of them were afraid, they walked with purpose. He hoped it was enough.

The children stopped outside the guild hall entrance where Khra's horse sniffed about, while Wolflock and Blandt joined Mothy and the tall stranger with the cloak.

"... And that's when I realised the importance of

toe hygiene. Never again, good sir. Never again. Oh! Lockie! Did you slay the scoundrel?"

Wolflock chuckled. "He's locked in the tomb. I thought it was a rather fitting place for his attitude and behaviour."

"Poetic. I like it. The ward went down a few minutes ago and our dummy is just ahead of us. We're waiting for it to move."

The stranger looked at Blandt with unblinking eyes. His brow furrowed in concern, and he opened his mouth, but he didn't speak. Wolflock saw that Blandt glanced at him several times before clearing his throat and looking everywhere for a scrap of conversation.

"Is it here yet?" one child called out.

"No," Blandt responded.

A few more moments went by. The bright stars littered the cloudless sky and the half-moon light edged higher.

"Is it here yet?"

"No."

Wolflock huffed. "We're going to need a water source. Volseggir has some magic pendant that turns it into blood. You're going to be thirsty after you bite it, and I am not fond of the idea of being a meal."

"Is it here yet?"

"No. There's an old fountain past the hall that way. It's meant to be for travellers, but Volseggir closed the road off. Or there are water troughs for the horses."

The stranger's jaw clenched, sounding like the snap of an alligator. "He has the bloodstone? And you expect Blandt to..." His red eyes widened, and he shook his head. "We won't be having that."

He turned on his heel and stalked towards the tomb.

"Is it here yet?"

"No."

"Did any of you pick up a red gemstone from the tomb or graveyard?"

Wolflock didn't receive an answer. They just mumbled among themselves. He sighed and made his way back to the carriage, wondering if he'd missed something on their maps. He had to move. The waiting was worse than having the attack.

"Is it here yet?"

Wolflock passed by the motionless Khra when he heard a wooden clinking sound.

"No. Not yet," Blandt called back.

He stopped and squinted at their driver. He'd never seen him move unaided. The black clad being had never spoken without his vampiric horse right next to his head. And the hook on the back of the driver's seat could easily be used to keep him in place.

Khra turned his broad-brimmed hat towards Wolflock in a slow, creaking motion.

As he lifted his head, Wolflock saw the collar of his jacket had the embroidered insignia for the Hunter's Guild. This was Blyrkjun's Samhain parade contribution from over forty that was meant to trap the bubak for the first time.

The cracked, featureless wooden face of the mannequin looked at Wolflock, stretching and testing its new fingers as it dropped the reigns.

"It's here!" Wolflock shouted and made a dash for the tombs towards the stranger.

He thought he had time until the black clothed monster shot over him, knocking him on his back. Blandt and Mothy ran forward, as did Tultra, brandishing the heated sword, but that didn't stop the bubak from looming over him.

Black smoke flooded out from under its duster jacket, obscuring their vision. Thunder rumbled from the direction of the guildhall. The bubak raised a leather gloved hand that reformed into a sharpened stake.

Wolflock pushed himself backwards, but he knew he couldn't get away from it in time. It was too powerful.

Too fast. It had fed off so much fear for decades. His brief glimmer of courage was nothing.

The thunder grew and Wolflock kept his eye directly on that blank face as he slid back onto his feet.

CRUNCH.

A black mass flew past him and the sound of wood breaking echoed around them. The black mare had the mannequin in her fangs. Her eyes grew brighter and brighter red as she snapped down on the throat of the bubak.

"K-Khra?" Wolflock swallowed.

Her eyes burned into his. The mannequin tried to reach up and pry her mouth off of it, but she just bit down harder. The black smoke evaporated as Mothy and Blandt looked on in great confusion. Finally, she spat out the empty shell of the mannequin.

"I... promised... Dorbi," she growled.

Wolflock approached her, hand extended for her to meet. He understood, now, why Khra sounded so strange. Horse vocalisations were a mixture of throaty growling and shrill notes. That's why the carriage had been poorly maintained except for the essentials. They hadn't paid coin because of that. That's why her shoes fit poorly. She couldn't ask for help.

"It's all fine. How... are you feeling?"

"I..." Her eyes bulged out of her head and her lips peeled back over her vicious white fangs. "... am sorry."

She snapped at his hand, then reared back, kicking out her lethal hooves. Wolflock ducked and scrambled away.

"Lockie, run!" Mothy screamed from behind them.

Wolflock vaulted the stable gate and slid through a side hutch, trying to get her slowed by the obstacles. Obstacles! That was it!

He turned sharply and raced towards the obstacle course. His heartbeat in his chest like a hammer as the hooves beating behind him gained speed. Khra let out a terrible horse scream, and he heard her snap behind him.

Just as he felt her hot breath on the back of his head, a sickening thump took it away. He looked over his shoulder to see the stranger collide with the ravenous horse, grasping her around the neck to try to restrain her.

"Run! You'll be safe at the tomb! I'll hold her here."

Wolflock didn't have to be told twice. He sprinted for the tomb, but, as he saw Volseggir's evil grin through the bars, he knew that wouldn't work. Cornered, he looked around. The gemstone had come off here, surely. He knew something had gotten caught in the sword. And only a few things could have made that distinct metal on stone sound.

A plume of bright purple fire sprung up in the distance to his right. With his legs trembling, he took one last gamble. He turned.

He heard the rumble of the hooves, the cries of the stranger, the shouts of his friends as he ran for the fountain. Retta stood next to it, her eyes blazing and her left hand holding the leather necklace with a huge red gemstone attached to it. Wolflock used every ounce of strength he could muster. He sprinted up that hill to the fountain and leaped.

He heard the rumble of the hooves stop as Khra leaped after him.

Then all he heard and felt was the splash of blood.

Rhiannon D. Elton

CHAPTER 11

A Case Satiated

Wolflock tried his best to keep his mouth closed as the red liquid flowed around him. He splashed to his feet, shaking his hands to flick the blood off with disgust etched across his face. He turned and saw Khra with both of her front legs in the fountain and her entire mouth and nose under the red liquid. Retta chuckled from the side, recognition coming back into her face.

Wolflock grumbled and got out of the fountain as the others caught up.

"You are the luckiest person I have ever met and, frankly, you're a danger to society," Mothy gasped, pulling Wolflock into a tight hug. "You smell terrible, but I don't mind. It's all fine. You're safe."

Wolflock held his arms out so as not to stain Mothy's shirt any more than it already had been.

"I'm fine. It all went according to plan. Mostly. Somewhat. Not at all."

Blandt snorted with laughter and clapped him on the back. "That was the boldest, but stupidest, thing I've ever seen. Well done. We'll be telling this story for years."

"How did all this happen?" the stranger shook his head, still watching Blandt carefully.

"Ah, where are my manners? I'm Blandt," said the young half vampire, holding out his hand to the older man.

"I know."

The pale boy looked confused.

"Blandt," Wolflock detached from Mothy and wiped his face down, "this is Blyrkjun Oviru. Your father."

The people gathered around looked dumbstruck.

"Lockie, you can't just say things like-" Mothy started.

"It wasn't hard to figure out, Mothy. Runar's notes and shrine gave us Blyrkjun's full name and, from

Blandt's birth certificate, we have confirmation of his marriage to Maret Anna, so, unless you have a brother-"

Blyrkjun shook his head, "I don't."

"-we have your father."

Blandt opened and closed his mouth a few times. "Why... why did you leave?"

Wolflock felt his bangle tugging his arm towards Creast harder.

"I... After we took out the bubak the night of your naming ceremony, I couldn't control myself. I nearly... I nearly bit your mother. When I left the inn to get some air and I..." he stroked Khra's back, "I bit my horse. I couldn't let her die, though. Not for my mistake. I turned her, but she couldn't go in the sunlight anymore. We had to live our lives in secret. I'm so sorry, girl." He took a breath and continued, "I saw the inn go up in flames and I couldn't do a thing. I thought you'd both died for years. I saw what Volseggir was doing in the province, and I tried to stop him, but I'm no good against fire. His weapon of choice became my weakness. Eventually, I think he had enough pressure on him that he was too scared to leave the guild property. He started sending the eldest off the property for errands. I saw him try his hand at hunting and helped him out a few times. Then I realised," he smiled with closed lips at Blandt, "that he was like me.

Just stronger."

Wolflock struggled to keep his arm by his side. The bangle pulled him.

"Can we discuss this inside? If Khra has her fill and it isn't me?"

Mothy saw him straining as the others chuckled and gripped the bangle, holding it down to help him. Khra finished her drinking and walked around the fountain until she found the bloodstone. She wiped her mouth on the grass and approached Wolflock with her head down.

"I... I am sorry." She whimpered.

Wolflock saw her eyes had gone back to black and that predatory energy was minimal. She could have resembled a normal horse. He reached out and stroked her neck.

"You couldn't help it. With that," he pointed at the gemstone she carried, "you won't be in a position where it will happen again. You got us this far in our journey. We couldn't have done it without you. You saved me from the bubak too. I'm just sorry you weren't able to tell us the truth until now."

She nudged him tenderly, snorting hot air on his arm. "I am... sorry."

She stayed by him all the way to the guildhall and

Blyrkjun threw open the doors with unnatural strength.

Blandt called the children to gather all their bedding and tear apart Volseggir's bed to add extra padding. They curled up together, opening all of Volseggir's private food stores, throwing the purple powder into the fire, and chatting with smiles on their faces.

Wolflock leaned against Khra's cool body and Mothy made jokes, never straying too far from him and helping him keep the bangle down, although it took both of their weight to keep it pinned. Wolflock just wanted to enjoy this moment of success and celebration before he resigned himself to failure.

As he looked around at the room, it didn't feel like a failure, though. The children laughed and ate at ease. Khra and the other vampires in Shiriling had a tool they could use to hurt no one again. The Hunters' Guild was freed from a troglodyte tyranny. He'd done a good thing.

Retta dragged her feet over to them and held out a bushel of soft spiky leaves for Mothy.

"What's this?" Wolflock asked as his friend gasped with delight.

"I told you Retta had her secrets."

Mothy stood up and brewed a hanging cauldron filled with wild lettuce and mint. Retta took his seat next to Wolflock and patted the bangle he struggled to keep down. Mothy made sure everyone drank the tea, especially Retta.

It numbed Wolflock's pains, and he relaxed, but the children and Blandt looked around as if they saw everything clearly for the first time in ages. Even Retta sat up straighter and wiped her hair out of her face, the cloudiness dissipating from her eyes.

The bangle jolted, and the ice grew around his wrist.

"I'm sorry, everyone. I may have to be involuntarily excused soon," he said, unable to stop the pewter band from rising into the air.

"Wolflock?" Blandt jumped to his feet.

"I wasn't able to solve the case. Old Finnes'Anna will have me back in Creast. Hopefully, this thing travels swiftly and up high. I don't particularly want to be dragged through the woods over the course of a week."

The room broke into a chorus of outrage but fell quiet as Retta waved her finger and the bangle held still. Thin purple flames gripped it in position and melted some of the ice away from his wrist.

"What part of your contract did you not fulfil?" she asked, slowly blinking up at him from her seat on the floor.

The firelight made her clear eyes sparkle orange and violet.

"I... uh..." her look felt so intense that he felt interrogated under her gaze, "I couldn't find out what happened to Maret'Anna Oviru."

Retta sipped her tea again and as if by magic, her wrinkles softened, her nose shrank, her lips filled and the muscles in her legs and arms filled. She didn't look like she was a hundred years old anymore. She looked far closer to five or six decades.

"A witch is only as young as her mind," she smacked her lips. "Let's see what my cold sister has done to you."

Wolflock stood, aghast. A second later, he heard Blandt run around the fire pit, but a whoosh of wind nearly knocked him over.

Blyrkjun reappeared from his shadow form with his arms around the old woman. He looked as if he were only in his early forties except for his red eyes, but they embraced as if it were their wedding day.

"Maret. Oh, my love. My patience. My beautiful Maret. How?" the vampire breathed, holding her cheek and lower back.

"It's only just starting to come back to me, my dear. I think I'll have more of that tea."

Blandt raced past Wolflock, whose bangle tried to drag him to the door.

"Mother?"

The room cheered as the family embraced, united once more.

"Uh... Sorry. A little help, Mrs Oviru?" Wolflock held onto the doorframe.

"Oh! Yes. My apologies." The old lady waved her finger and the purple flames pulled him forward again. Sparks flew by him and after a few seconds the tin box, Runar's diary, and Volseggir's papers surrounded the room like a spinning night light casting shapes across the walls and ceiling. "Please, I would very much like to hear the tale. From the beginning."

Wolflock's shoulders relaxed in relief as the flames fought the bangle, letting him use his arm normally. "Mothy and I missed our transport to Mystentine, so we employed the services of Khra, who we believed at the time to be the driver, not the horse. To pay for our journey, we had to agree with the demands of Finnes'Anna of Creast. She sent us to find out what happened to her sister, Maret, and her husband, Runar. She believed they had run off together and that the appearance of her husband's carriage would lead us to the right clues."

Blyrkjun shook his head, clasping Maret's hand and patting his son on the shoulder. "Runar was the most honourable man I ever knew. He would never abandon his family. That's why he was always so torn. He wanted the family he knew in Veidimenn Deild to reach their fullest potential and also to keep his wife happy."

Wolflock nodded. "He found the library under the guild hall. A place that had been long forgotten by the guild members. He used it to make the region safer and happier. He worked with the local witches and taught the locals how they could defend themselves. Volseggir hated this; it lost the guild profits, and he couldn't extort the locals. In fact, he began letting the same monsters the guild protected the people from kill them so he could claim their land. His methods made Runar question his allegiances, which drove him to Creast with Finnes'Anna."

Wolflock pointed to the diary and other documents. When he pointed, they flew down and displayed themselves for everyone to read as they floated by.

"While he was too far away, they sent Blyrkjun to fend off a vampire nest and he became infected. Maret helped your wounds heal, but you would never be the same. Runar discovered what you were, but he never told a soul. He didn't want to risk you being hurt."

"I still ache to this day that I couldn't do the same for him," the vampire sighed, resting his head on his wife's shoulder.

"Ah, but the odds were stacked against you. On the night of your wedding, while everyone was celebrating, you three lured a bubak into a trap and destroyed it. I'm sure you wanted to show your friend that your new powers could be useful to the guild, but Volseggir found out what you were doing. Runar had confronted him only a short while prior to his misdealings. He knew he had to eliminate him. In the night's dark he crept up and killed Runar while you trapped the bubak. I have seen firsthand that he doesn't like to fight people to their face unless they are smaller and weaker than him."

"How do you know it wasn't the bubak?" one child asked, enamoured upon the tale.

"Because Runar wasn't afraid. He was very confident. The trap had gone perfectly. You both knew it too, though, didn't you?" He looked to Maret and Blyrkjun, who nodded sadly. "That's why, when you made your shrine to him in the cave near Restöfundsjúkum, you marked your names as ones to avenge him."

"We worked tirelessly, but, with Volseggir as guild

master, we couldn't openly question him. The people who did were dishonoured from the guild, but we would not let the land suffer," Blyrkjun filled in the gap.

"Then thirty years ago, on the day of your son's naming ceremony, another bubak attacked. Blyrkjun killed it, but, without Maret's magical bloodstone, he was left hungry."

"I had to step outside. And that's when I saw-"

"Me," Khra snorted and bobbed her head.

"You underestimated your thirst, though, and drained her. You couldn't bear to lose your faithful steed, and, so, you transformed her into the vampire horse we see today. While this happened, Volseggir used his heat sword to cut down the tree outside the inn while also setting it on fire. It would look like an accident to the untrained eye, but it was meant to kill his biggest adversaries. Both of you and your new son."

"I thought you had perished in the fire." Maret held back a sob.

"And I thought you had, as well. I never returned to the guild after that night."

"I moved into the guild to keep a closer eye on Volseggir and make sure our son trained enough to be able to protect himself from the monster."

Wolflock interrupted by pointing at the unclaimed

adoption papers and land deeds. "You both sabotaged his efforts. You both helped the people of the region and slowed his progress. It only hindered your success in stopping him when he employed the services of a criminal by the name of Astraxis, who supplied him with a powerful herb that could control the will of the people he used it on."

"He put it in all the children's soup and said it was Retta's- I mean mother's medicine." Blandt looked horrified.

"It slows the mind and dulls the senses. Eventually, he did the one thing Astraxis told him not to do, which was to feed it to people. I don't believe Astraxis ever witnessed the effects it had on a witch." Wolflock continued.

Mothy refilled her tea. "I'm so sorry for all you've been through. It was your notes that helped us find the cure, though. You said to use wild lettuce, and it's working."

"What would drive a man to be so vile?" Blandt asked, shaking his head.

"Volseggir dreamed of taking over the region with an enormous fortress. He knew things weren't going to plan, and so he grew paranoid. Guild members left, and your mother was the only one who stayed. He became so paranoid that, even when new people wanted to join, he would refuse to let them train or hunt. Once people came onto the property, they weren't allowed to leave. He tried to keep his terrible grasp over everything in his life with not an ounce of honour or a shred of decency. He thought he had controlled Maret, but she slipped into moments of lucidness. She knew the place where she sent vampires to drink in safety had been compromised, so she asked Blandt to destroy the note that redirected them to here, where Volseggir had stolen the bloodstone."

"What a greedy, filthy, lying scum-" Blyrkjun balled his fists in rage.

"Love, calm down. There are children here. Mind your language." Maret kissed his pale cheek and he relaxed.

Wolflock stretched his neck and as all the papers settled into a neat pile by the kitchen, he moved his fingers to the bangle. "And there we have it. Case solved."

"Wait!" Maret reached out, her magic catching his fingers. "One last thing." The purple flames transformed into the shape of a pen and along the pewter, she wrote:

I am so sorry. All will be explained soon. I love you, my sister. I will see you soon.

And in an explosion of snowflakes that sounded like a shattering mirror, the bangle disappeared.

Without a worry in their hearts, the children, the Ovirus, Khra, Mothy and Wolflock rested around the warm embers of the firepit under the protection of the ancient warriors carved into the beams above them.

The boys slept late the next day, knowing they wouldn't be leaving until nightfall, anyway. Maret and Blyrkjun set about their work, making sure the children were bathed and dressed, as well as taking inventory of their food, medicine and cleaning supplies. The old vampire did all his work inside.

Blandt slept through the day and the children played with toys they made with Mothy and read any of the books they wanted to from the library.

When Wolflock did wake, he chatted with Khra, leaning on her side. He asked her about what it was like to be a vampiric horse and what she remembered from her living life. He didn't want her to feel alone.

"What are you going to do after you've finished your task with us?" he asked, nursing a cup of the dandelion tea Mothy insisted he take after a bath to get the fountain blood off of him and while his clothes were washed.

"I will return here. Blyr needs me. I had been so scared the night I turned that I ran and couldn't find my way back. Then... I forgot."

"I'm sure it will be much better than your cave."

"Yes. I will not have to clean the carriage," she nickered with a laugh.

The sun set later that day and they set off again after a long goodbye.

"Go on then." Blandt punched Wolflock gently in the shoulder. "Get off my turf. clever cleats."

"I was right." Wolflock chuckled.

"That will be the last time you're ever allowed to say that to me."

"I was still right. May your hunts be the best of your life. Merry part, Blandt Oviru."

"And merry meet again, Wolflock. Study well."

They nodded their understanding to one another, and Khra set off down the lane and back onto the main road. The two boys didn't have to like one another to respect each other.

Wolflock and Mothy slept soundly for the last two days of their journey and realised that the nightmares only came while Khra was hungry.

On the final evening of their journey, Wolflock felt the air change. He woke to the smell of smoke. The sky through the spotless window was layered from a starry dark blue with a soft ginger creeping up. The smoke he smelled came from chimneys, and, as he propped himself up to get a better look, the sight of hundreds of houses down the way from them met his eye. Their rickety, mismatched rooftops made it look like art. His heart soared, and he leaped to Mothy, shaking him awake.

"Mothy! Mothy, look!"

His friend opened his groggy eyes, and they looked up together at the giant mountain on the edge of Mystentine City.

Wolflock smiled as he glanced from Mothy to the window. "I'm not going to lie. I'm glad we missed that carriage."

The Case of the Haematophagous Equine

Rhiannon D. Elton

Finnes'Anna's Curse

Vid is vin dinn og sno ji
Sál pín mun ge fa mér gaum.
Bin did med ban og med togi
Ord pitt er skylt ad pet vaum.
Med og med ljoma halfs sins
Bekking Magret Anna og Runar Slatra skalt pú pekkja.
Settu pinna og snudu honum hreinum
Eg skal vita allt sem pu hefur sed.

By the ice wind and snow
Your very soul will pay me heed.
Bind by bracelet and by tow
Your word is bound to do this deed.
By and by the half-moon's glow
the knowledge of Magret Anna and Runar Slatra, you shall
know.
Place the pin and turn it clean
I shall know all you have seen.

Dire Myna,

I bin nicht stellan I wirst es fähig zu schreib zu sa
atonen. I habe lthen untersuchet sein Rhea und them
pferd zu ringen state lather zu sa ein der extreme
sein nicht ablesen. I habe nur getötelet zat ein
furchtbarch finsterist gähren der gepetchen hinge
mirena und I tun nicht relexen sich befugnisaft is
sas his furzsich.

Es is ein sele menant Uorxaris wirt is am der hentra
sein ischeret. I sa nicht kennt aus them vinalig komplett
is, aber I glaube is is zwigas weitem grxbrobist als
hurs ein tell sein serbest pichln schluerlt und
mertelteam stulberx. Uf sa za sazu ein sagenet den
purett stulber ein neulich leuten fische, habe sein
strotnahm umittelbarich. Slich sah der panze Ichau
Gedanken behorrsh. Dat wirst mittielen sa ischeret sa
besarf.

I bin taurchuslgung I habe nur za retzenet. Bitte slich
fumf mich am der Iägrine Zunft zwich Grxast und
Mystentine, und fumf der Dutze gegan, sa nicht glaube
ein sstabel Belesgor zagen.

Dine brother,

Bolflich I. Folen

N.S. Di wirst za recht durch them. I kennt sa wirst.

N.N.S. I surstsis. Alle is gut. I wirst schreib atonen
gebnet I bin am Mystentine.

About the Author

Rhiannon is the walker between worlds. One foot in Earth, the other constantly stepping into Pelaia. As if gazing into a crystal ball, she sees this other world and all that happens within it with the clarity of someone staring through a veil. It is her purpose in life to transcribe these histories, adventures and mysteries for you to enjoy.

This witchy woman was raised by a fairy who taught her that there are all kinds of magic throughout the world. She taught Rhiannon to withhold judgement because you never truly know another's story. She also taught her that everyone, no matter how flawed, has something to give.

The adventures of Rhiannon's youth lead her through trials and dangers that taught her about the darkness within the world, but it also showed her that anything could be overcome. There was always a way. Surrounded by so much apathy and hopelessness, Rhiannon made it her goal in life to show others the light and that if they could dream it they could do it.

The way she was shown this was through stories.

Stories of friendship, love, adventure, discovery, compassion, understanding, and kindness. All of these stories gave her new friends, new lessons, new life.

In the depths of her darkest place during year 11 and 12, when she felt at her loneliest, drugs surrounded her life in terrible ways, the self worth of those she loved and admired crumbled, she was relentlessly bullied and felt friendless in her most trying years, she lived in squalor due to bureaucratic errors, and yet she still had to be "perfect". She had to perfectly excel in school, she had to perfectly remain calm and gentle in the face of abusive men, she had to be a perfect role model for all those around her. That craving for perfection in order to get love nearly killed her several times. In all of this darkness with politicians sacrificing real people and real environments for imaginary money, with teachers displaying no compassion for their students, with men abusing women and children, with communities vilifying those who needed them most, with injustice reigning and all hope seemingly lost... Puinteyle was born.

All of these pains in life were fixed in Puinteyle.

All of them were able to be mended and healed because of a conscientious effort. The people of Puinteyle wanted to be better than their problems. Puinteyle was where people made an effort to love freely and always sought to help each other, animals and the environment. Harmony. True and beautiful harmony. Where the pendulum never swayed too far away from that beautiful harmonious and happy point of balance.

But like in our lives, there is always obstacles to overcome and darkness to understand. Therefore, Puinteyle would always have its own inner turmoils to learn and grow from too. Thus, the stories never truly end.

Rhiannon has always lived and breathed stories, knowing her role in life is to be this guide through a new world for others. Her dream is to support her community with her stories, as well as creating a company where other artists can come together in celebration of Pelaia and all it has to offer.

Become Part of the Magic & Mystery...

www.patreon.com/RhiDElton

If you want more clues, more magic and more mystery, support me on Patreon.

You'll get exclusive clues, maps, sketches, behind the scenes stories, lore and much more! You'll also be the first to know when a new story is coming out so you can solve the mystery before your friends.

If you join at any tier above $10 you can get mugs, posters, bags and shirts, all with your favourite characters.

www.patreon.com/RhiDElton

Stay tuned for the next mystery in the series:

THE WOLFLOCK CASES

BOOK 9

THE CASE OF THE LOST ANTRUM

www.rhiannoneltonauthor.com

 RhiDElton

 RhiannonEltonAuthor

 RhiDElton

 rhiannoneltonauthor

 Rhiannon D. Elton

 RhiDElton

THE WOLFLOCK CASES

1. The Case of the Captain's Hair

2. The Case of Mothy

3. The Case of the Curse of Houl

4. The Case of the Bitter Draught

5. The Study in Silver

6. The Case of the Lost Mermaid

7. The Case of the Pisces Moon

8. The Case of the Haematophagous Equine

9. The Case of the Lost Antrum

10. The Case of the Mountain's Monster

www.ingramcontent.com/pod-product-compliance
Lightning Source LLC
Chambersburg PA
CBHW020404120726
47904CB00002B/702